MORE COMMON SENSE

MORE COMMON SENSE

To Wendy
Thank you
Colin Wreford
15/9/23

COLIN WREFORD

This is a work of fiction. Names, characters, businesses, places, events and incidents are either the products of the author's imagination or used in a fictitious manner. Any resemblance to actual persons, living or dead, or actual events is purely coincidental.

Matador
Unit E2 Airfield Business Park,
Harrison Road, Market Harborough,
Leicestershire. LE16 7WB
Tel: 0116 2792299
Email: books@troubador.co.uk
Web: www.troubador.co.uk/matador
Twitter: @matadorbooks

ISBN 978 1 80514 119 8

British Library Cataloguing in Publication Data.
A catalogue record for this book is available from the British Library.

Printed and bound in Great Britain by 4edge Limited
Typeset in 12pt Minion Pro by Troubador Publishing Ltd, Leicester, UK

Matador is an imprint of Troubador Publishing Ltd

I dedicate this book to my late parents Jack and Betty and to Abby who can make me laugh even when I don't feel like laughing.

CHAPTER 1

INSPECTOR MELVILLE

April 2034

It is about ten minutes after Sara Molan is removed to hospital before Deputy Commissioner Giles arrives at the scene.

"Where is the Prime Minister?"

"At Rochester Row, Ma'am. The victim is at Chelsea and Westminster. I've got officers inside and outside the hospital. I've asked for updates on her condition every thirty minutes."

"What are her chances?"

"Not good, not at all good. She's lost a huge amount of blood, but she was still alive when she left here thanks to Sergeant Adams."

"Take me through what has gone on here tonight, Inspector."

"The Prime Minister left instructions that no one was

to enter this floor tonight. I understand that the victim, Sara Molan, came up here to conduct an interview. She handed over her phone and bag at the police barrier on the PM's orders. There is recording equipment in another room being examined by Forensics which appears to contain film of an interview between the two of them. The switchboard here got a phone call just before nine saying someone was in danger in the PM's quarters. It was a woman with an accent, possibly European. We came straight up here and could hear a female screaming as soon as we entered the floor. I banged on the door and Mr Godwin told me to go away, so we kicked the door in. The victim was lying on the floor to the left of the door and the Prime Minister was over by the food, naked and holding a bloodstained knife. The PM said he loved her, had asked her to marry him and he couldn't remember what happened after that."

"Have you arrested him?"

"No, Ma'am. He is helping us with our enquiries."

"Do the press know?"

"Not to my knowledge, but we won't keep this quiet for long especially with the number of police deployed here and at the hospital."

"Right, well, we will wait until morning and hope nothing leaks earlier. Try to find the woman who made that call and speak to Sara's boss about why she was here on her own in the Prime Minister's private quarters. Then visit the Speaker of the House of Commons and tell him, in strictest confidence, what is going on. I'll meet you at Rochester Row at ten AM tomorrow to interview the Prime Minister together," Deputy Commissioner Giles says as she sweeps towards the exit, leaving Melville muttering to himself. "Thank you for everything you've done, Inspector, and make sure you get plenty of sleep."

Having had his private moan, the Inspector goes into the room where the interview took place and asks the Forensic team for their latest news. "What's on the tape?"

"An interview between the Prime Minister and Sara Molan. From what we've seen so far, he seems to be doing virtually all the talking and she seems nervous and unhappy," says the Forensics Officer.

"Anything else I should know?"

"We found her things in the PM's bedroom. She made three calls early this evening according to the numbers in memory. The first was to William Marshall. The second to David McDougall which only lasted five seconds, suggesting it went straight to voicemail, and the third to an unlisted mobile."

"I need all three of those numbers."

"Yes, sir."

Five minutes later, Inspector Melville is in his own office in Downing Street and carefully dialling the mysterious mobile number called by Sara Molan before she entered the Prime Minister's private rooms. After a few rings, a sleepy-sounding female voice answers. "Bonsoir."

"Parlez vous Anglais?" asks Melville hesitantly.

"Yes," replies the voice on the other end. "How can I help you?"

"My name is Inspector Melville of the Metropolitan Police in London. To whom am I speaking?"

"I am Nicolette Du Bois."

"Did you speak to a lady called Sara Molan earlier this evening?"

"Oui."

"Can I ask your relationship with Ms Molan, please?"

"We used to be life partners but split up about five years ago. We have been back in contact for a year or so."

"Where are you based?"

"Marseilles. Inspector, you are worrying me. Has something happened to Sara?"

"I'm afraid it has, Ms Du Bois. We found her injured in Downing Street tonight. She is currently in hospital."

"Injured. How?"

"We are still investigating that. I need to know why she rang you earlier."

"Sara asked me to phone a number she gave me at nine o'clock your time and tell whoever answered the telephone that someone was in danger in the Prime Minister's rooms. I was to make sure they investigated urgently before ending the call. I did just as she asked."

"Do you know why she wanted you to do that?"

"They wouldn't let her take her telephone in. She

said her boss was supposed to do it, but he swanned out. She was worried the Prime Minister was expecting her to sleep with him and she wanted to get away before he started coming on to her. What has happened? Is she alright?"

"Sara has been stabbed twice. She has lost a lot of blood. She is alive but critical and unconscious."

"Sacré bleu. I must be with her. I will catch the first flight to London."

"Please ring this number back when you have booked a flight. One of my officers will meet you and take you to the hospital. After that they will take you to Westminster police station so I can talk to you in detail about the conversation and how Sara has seemed recently."

"She feared Godwin. I think he was threatening to expose our relationship unless Sara did exactly what he wanted."

"I take it your relationship was secret?"

"It was private. Sara did not want her personal life plastered over the front pages. We had planned to marry until Godwin banned all same-sex partnerships. We could not marry and we split up, but we were trying to get back together. Inspector, I do not need your officers to take me around London. I lived there for five years."

"Nevertheless, you will have a police escort. Your ex-girlfriend has been savagely attacked and until I have arrested someone, you need to be protected. Ring when you know your flight. Au revoir."

Inspector Melville puts the phone down and thinks to himself, "That's interesting. No wonder she tried to beat him off. Not her type at all. Now for the Speaker."

*

Ten minutes later, Melville and Sergeant Adams arrive at Speakers House, directly underneath Big Ben. The Inspector explains to the police officer at the security barrier that he must talk to the Speaker immediately. Shortly afterwards, Melville and Adams are shown into the Speaker's private apartment. The Speaker, George Montague, emerges in his dressing gown shortly after their arrival, "What is the meaning of this intrusion at this ungodly hour? Even politicians are allowed sleep."

Inspector Melville is tempted to reply with a remark about his own lack of rest but instead says, "I'm sorry, but there has been an incident tonight and you need to be aware of it before the press find out. Earlier this evening, a young lady was found critically injured in the Prime Minister's private quarters in Downing Street. Mr Godwin was found naked in the room and holding a bloodstained knife. He is currently being held at Westminster police station whilst we try to work out exactly what has occurred."

"Well, he must be released immediately," replies the Speaker.

"That will not be happening, sir. The Prime Minister

will be interviewed later this morning and a decision will be made then as to whether he is prosecuted or released."

"The PM must attend the Dissolution of Parliament. It is essential he is present. Tradition. That is what is important."

"No, sir. Dealing with crime and apprehending the guilty is what is important. You will have to hold the Dissolution without Mr Godwin, I'm afraid. You will have to tell MPs that he is unavailable. I will let you know when you can make an official statement to Parliament. My Deputy Commissioner wants to keep this out of the media until we can establish whether a crime has taken place. We are expecting your full co-operation here. Hopefully, there will be a simple, lawful explanation and we can all get back to normal, but there could potentially be a massive scandal if Mr Godwin has deliberately injured the victim. Do I have your full co-operation?"

"Yes, in the circumstances I will wait for your permission to inform members of the situation but—"

Mr Montague is interrupted immediately by the Inspector, "No buts, sir. If you have any complaints, please take them up with the Deputy Commissioner's office."

"Be assured, I will. Now, if there is nothing else, I am going back to bed. You will be hearing from me in the morning."

*

After a few hours of dozing in his Downing Street office, Inspector Melville summons Sergeant Adams and they head out again to speak to William Marshall at the TV station.

Sara's boss isn't particularly pleased to see them, "This had better be quick. I can't contact Sara, Godwin or even the technicians working on the interview tape. I've got a programme to get on air in four hours' time and I have nothing. Fuck all."

The Inspector takes a deep breath and begins, "Do you know where Sara Molan was last evening?"

"With the Prime Minister in Downing Street recording the interview for today's show, of course. An interview I haven't got, naturally."

"And afterwards?"

"No idea."

"Did Sara Molan ask you to contact her last night so she could use the call as an excuse to get away from the PM?"

"Look, what the hell is going on here? I haven't got time for this," says Mr Marshall, as he half rises from his chair.

"Please sit down, sir. Were you supposed to ring Ms Molan last night or not?"

"Yes, but I told her I couldn't do it."

"Why not, sir?"

"Just tell me what is going on here."

"Alright, Sara Molan was critically injured last night and is in hospital. She was stabbed twice. Now, that information is subject to a broadcast embargo at the moment and if you mention it in your programme I will have you in a cell before you can say 'Scoop'. Got it?"

"Yes," Mr Marshall's irritation shows through in his curt reply.

"Now why did you refuse to help her get away from Godwin last night?"

"Because Godwin rang me and told me not to try to contact her or disrupt the interview in any way. He has some information about me which I would prefer stayed out of the public arena."

"So, he blackmailed you into leaving Ms Molan to her own devices?"

"He has something on her, as well."

"Yes, I know about that. What the hell were you doing sending a young female presenter into the private quarters of a blackmailer who was obsessed with her?"

"I didn't think she was at any risk. He only wanted to fuck her. All she had to do was close her eyes and think of India for a few minutes and it would have been over and done with. Why couldn't the silly bitch just open her legs? Now I've no interview, no presenter and no programme."

"Ms Molan's ex, Nic, is flying in later. I'll introduce you and then maybe you will understand why your employee was terrified of being alone with Godwin and why she needed your help. By the way, the police have the interview tape and, believe me, you are not missing anything at all by not screening it. I will send an officer round to take a full statement from you. If I hear of any lack of co-operation from you, I will turn your life upside down until I find out exactly what Godwin had on you, whether it is relevant to this case or not. I hope that is clear enough for you."

On his way back to his car, Inspector Melville mutters to Sergeant Adams, "Didn't even ask how she is or which hospital she is in."

Turning his phone back on, he discovers a missed call from the team at Westminster police station. He rings them immediately. "Melville here, someone wants me."

"Yes, sir. The victim has been taken back into theatre. She appears to be bleeding internally. Ms Du Bois is arriving at one fifteen this afternoon and the Deputy Commissioner wants you back here at ten o'clock to start interviewing the Prime Minister."

"Keep me posted on Ms Molan. Get an officer to meet that flight and take Ms Du Bois to the hospital and then to me. I'm on my way back, so the interview is no problem. Can you get someone to the TV station to get a statement from William Marshall? He's slippery and frantically trying to protect his own back, so send someone who can tell the difference between truth and crap."

"Yes, sir. Oh, one more thing. The Deputy Commissioner says King Charles wants to announce what has happened. He's going to give a press briefing at three o'clock at Buckingham Palace, so there are to be no leaks before that."

"Just great. Get one of the Sergeants at Downing Street to ring George Montague, the House of Commons Speaker, and tell him that he can make an announcement after the King has had his say. He will not be a happy bunny so just tell him the facts and leave him to his rant."

"Yes, sir."

*

It is just after nine thirty when Melville arrives back at the police station. The Custody Sergeant calls to him as he enters, "Godwin has got his brief with him. Some bloke called Benge from Mayfair. When you're ready to start, I'll let them know."

"Do you know this Benge?"

"Never seen him before in my life. We don't get many here who know anyone in Mayfair."

Before the Inspector can move away, Deputy Commissioner Giles enters. Ignoring the reception desk, she walks straight over to Melville and speaks, "We need to find an empty office and you can update me on what is happening before the interview." They borrow the Duty Inspector's office and, once settled, she asks, "How did you get on?"

"Well, I think I understand the background to this a lot better. I spoke to the victim's ex-partner, Nic, whose full name is Nicolette Du Bois. She's flying in at one fifteen. I'm arranging a car to take her to the hospital and then bring her here. She says Ms Molan was terrified of Godwin, which is why Nic agreed to phone Downing Street to give her a means of escape. He blackmailed Sara into doing the interview alone in the evening. Nic thinks he was threatening to expose their relationship."

"So, Sara rang her former girlfriend for help?"

"Yes, Ma'am. Originally, she asked her boss, William Marshall, to make the call. He 'swanned out' as Nic put it which presumably means he ducked out of it. Godwin blackmailed him into agreeing to the interview in the first place and then ordered him not to contact Ms Molan that evening. He's hiding something but at this stage he is probably a key witness, so we may have to turn a blind eye for the moment."

"Do you think Godwin knew that Sara Molan is gay? I cannot imagine him wanting to marry a lesbian."

"Well, if he didn't then there must be something else he knows about her and at the moment I have no idea what that could be."

"Do we know how many people knew about Nic's gender?"

"She said the relationship was totally private. I haven't told Marshall, but I'm convinced he doesn't know. I'm planning to take Nic over to the studio and introduce her. See who is surprised and who isn't."

"My office has had three calls from George Montague already. Has he been told about the King's briefing?"

"Yes, Ma'am. That should generate even more calls. Mr Tradition is not a big fan of the monarchy, I believe."

"Quite so. Or the police. He is probably raising a mounted army of MPs led by Black Rod to storm this place and drag the PM off to dissolve Parliament. Right, let us get this interview underway. You can lead. We will hear what he has got to say and then adjourn to consider what, if any, charges we want to bring."

Five minutes later, Inspector Melville, Deputy Commissioner Giles, Prime Minister Robert "Bob" Godwin and solicitor Peregrine Benge are sitting on opposite sides of a large desk in interview room three.

Mr Benge opens the conversation, "I have a statement my client has prepared which he wishes me to read out. 'This is a personal statement of Robert "Bob" Godwin of Downing Street, London, given freely to the Metropolitan Police to assist in the investigation of the injuries sustained by Sara Molan. I had invited Ms Molan to my personal apartment in order to conduct an interview. She arrived shortly after seven thirty, we exchanged small talk and then went into another room to conduct the interview. That was a triumph and we returned to the original room to celebrate. Ms Molan had at least three glasses of champagne and no food. I had two drinks and ate some of the delicious ham. I then asked Ms Molan to marry me. She refused and said she still loved her ex, Nic. We then started to have sex and I pulled down her skirt. I jokingly ripped up her tights because I had asked her to wear stockings. I then pulled her panties down and started to kiss her and attempted to penetrate her. Suddenly she pushed me away and started screaming at me that I didn't know anything about her or Nic. She was hysterical and I admit I hit her to calm her down. Then she ran to the door, which was locked, and started screaming for help. I pulled her away from the door. The next thing I remember is someone outside in the corridor shouting for the door to be opened. The door was broken down and police officers entered. Sara was on the floor and she was bleeding. I was holding a knife because I wanted some more of the wonderful ham. I have no recollection of stabbing Ms Molan but there was no one else in the locked room, so somehow between Sara and myself she must have been accidentally stabbed in one of the struggles.' My client is not prepared to answer any questions whatsoever and refers you solely to the sequence of events detailed in his statement."

Inspector Melville remains silent for a few seconds and then starts to speak, "I would like to clarify one or two things about the statement. Would your client be prepared to discuss some aspects of his statement in greater detail?"

A whispered conversation takes place between Mr Godwin and Mr Benge. When that discussion finishes, Mr Benge replies, "You can raise some points, but I cannot guarantee that I will allow my client to answer."

"Fine. I will start with an easy point, Mr Godwin. What gender do you think Ms Molan's ex-partner, Nic, is?"

There is a further whispered discussion before the Prime Minister answers. "What a ridiculous question.

I am quite happy to answer that even if it is a massive waste of time. Nic is male, of course. Short for Nicholas, I guess."

Inspector Melville and Deputy Commissioner Giles exchange glances before the Inspector responds, "I have spoken to Nic in Marseilles. Nic is actually short for Nicolette and she is flying into Heathrow later today. I have reason to believe that you were coercing Ms Molan to undertake the interview on your terms because you were threatening to reveal details of her relationship. Yet you did not even know that she was homosexual. Did you really, as Prime Minister, want to marry a lesbian when you have been persecuting the gay community for the last five years?"

"Do not answer that," snaps Mr Benge. "No more questions. Charge my client or release him immediately."

Deputy Commissioner Giles speaks for the first time, "Prime Minister, did you discover that Sara was gay and is that why you stabbed her?"

"Enough," shouts the solicitor.

"Very well," responds Deputy Commissioner Giles, without even a glance at her colleague. "Robert Godwin, it is my decision to charge you with the attempted murder of Sara Molan and the attempted rape of Sara Molan. Inspector, will you please take Mr Godwin and Mr Benge to the Custody Sergeant and oversee the formal issuing of the charges. Mr Godwin, it is my intention for you to appear before a Magistrates Court later today. I will instruct the prosecutor to oppose bail."

"*This is preposterous*," bellows Mr Benge. "You cannot seriously charge and imprison our ruling Prime Minister. I will do whatever is necessary to arrange bail. You cannot send a Prime Minister who has introduced harsh sentences and punishments to a prison full of men with grudges against him. It is inhuman."

"Just like branding and shooting at dawn, then," says Inspector Melville and earns himself an ice-cold stare from the Deputy Commissioner, "Please come with me, gentlemen."

*

Prime Minister Robert "Bob" Godwin appears before Westminster Magistrates Court a few hours later and is remanded in custody. Mr Benge immediately goes to a higher court to secure his client's release. At five PM, Inspector Melville arrives at the Old Bailey for an emergency hearing before Justice Menzies to determine whether the defendant should be released on bail.

Inspector Melville is asked to present the police case for remand, "The facts of this case are simple. The defendant and the victim were together in a locked room. When I broke down the door to gain entry, Ms Sara Molan was lying half naked on the floor and bleeding profusely from what has now been proved to be two separate knife wounds. Mr Godwin was standing at the other side of the room holding a bloodstained carving knife. Forensic tests are not yet complete but the blood on the knife matches the victim's, the only fingerprints on the knife are the defendant's and preliminary tests indicate that Ms Molan's wounds are consistent with incisions made by the carving knife. This is a very serious matter, and it is not totally beyond the realms of possibility that Mr Godwin could, in due course, be further charged with murder. He is a man of power with influential friends and must be considered a flight risk. At present it appears that the defendant coerced Ms Molan and another person to set up the scenario leading to the attempted rape and violent assault on the victim. They need to be protected from the defendant and his associates. In the overall circumstances, the police and the prosecutor in this case believe that to avoid the defendant's disappearance and to protect the victim and potential witnesses, Mr Godwin should be remanded in custody forthwith."

"Thank you, Inspector," says Judge Menzies. "Mr Benge. I would like to hear your views on this situation now. An address similar in length to the Inspector's would be ideal."

"Your Honour, as you are fully aware, bail must be granted unless certain serious circumstances apply. The first test for remand is the nature of the offence. Attempted murder and attempted rape are serious charges which would normally lead to remand. However, in this case, the defendant cannot clearly remember how Ms Molan was injured but he definitely did not set out to hurt her. He proclaims his love for the victim and, at worst, this is a momentary lapse of control, a true crime of passion. My client has no previous convictions, has never been on bail, let alone broken bail, and there is no reason at all to think for a second that he is about to commit further offences. Finally, he has no intention of escaping justice and is willing to surrender his passport to the court. Mr Godwin has been Prime Minister of this country for five years. He is well known to the entire population and the idea that he could hide from the police is ridiculous. Therefore, I contend that he clearly passes the four tests. In my view, he has been overcharged by the police. The sexual contact between Mr Godwin and Ms Molan was consensual and a charge of assault would be far more appropriate than one of attempted murder. This matter is not as serious as the present charges indicate and I consider the first test has been met along with the other provisions for bail."

"Thank you, Mr Benge. Eloquent as usual and mercifully brief."

Inspector Melville rises, "Your Honour, I would like to offer some further clarification on some of Mr Benge's points, if I may."

"The floor is yours, Inspector."

"Firstly, Ms Molan is unconscious and has undergone two operations to deal with her injuries and subsequent internal bleeding. She is critically ill, and her survival is not guaranteed. To dismiss the attack as a minor assault case does not tally with the damage caused to the victim. Secondly, I have spoken to a third party who received a phone call from Ms Molan shortly before she went into Downing Street to meet the Prime Minister. That person tells me that Sara was terrified of the defendant and arranged for my witness to telephone Downing Street to provide Ms Molan with an opportunity to escape before Mr Godwin could sexually abuse her."

Mr Benge rises, "Your Honour, who is this mysterious witness being pulled out of the hat like a toy rabbit?"

"Inspector. Please reveal all."

"Yes, Your Honour. Mr Benge, in fact, already knows who this witness is. Ms Molan was previously in a relationship with the witness, Ms Nicolette Du Bois, usually known as Nic. She has flown in today from Marseilles and is currently at the hospital. She will then be interviewed and make a formal statement. Nic has told me over the telephone that Ms Molan is homosexual and was terrified that Mr Godwin would force her to have sex with him. The statement made just now by Mr Benge that sexual activity was consensual is rendered speculative at best by the undeniable facts that Sara Molan does not have relationships with men and was very aware that the Prime Minister intended her to spend the night with him and engage in heterosexual activity. Your Honour, there is a lot of pulling still to be done on the piece of string which is this case. I ask that the defendant be remanded in custody pending his trial to allow vital ongoing enquiries to take place unhindered."

"Thank you once again, Inspector," Judge Menzies

pauses and looks down at his notes before continuing. “I can see merit in many of Mr Benge’s points. At the moment, of course, we only have one side of the story, apart from small pieces of the jigsaw from the minor players. Based on what has been presented to this court, I must agree with Inspector Melville that Mr Benge’s assertion that sex was consensual is highly speculative in view of the victim’s currently illegal sexual preferences. I disagree with you, Mr Benge, that your client passes the first test. Ms Molan has been grievously injured and the fact that she is currently unconscious in hospital tells me that this is a serious matter. As such, the defendant fails the criteria for automatic bail. I, of course, have discretion to grant bail due to my seniority and many years of dealing with scum who cannot tell the difference between a human being and a punchbag. I do not feel inclined to use discretion here and I remand the defendant to prison pending further court hearings.”

Mr Benge rises and addresses the judge, “Your Honour, it is simply not safe for my client to be imprisoned with criminals who have been adversely affected by his harsh additions to the penal code and sentencing guidelines. If you feel unable to grant bail, then could you please consider specific measures to protect Mr Godwin during his stay in prison?”

“I would have expected your client to welcome the opportunity to see first-hand what effect his reforms have had on those unfortunate enough to be convicted in the last five years. I am sure there will be no shortage of inmates more than willing to show him the whip marks on their backs or the brandings on their foreheads. Mr Godwin's protection is a matter for the prison authorities, but I will recommend to them that he should be kept apart from other prisoners whenever possible to prevent attacks on his person. That concludes matters as far as I am concerned. Officers, please take the prisoner down."

As the court clears, Deputy Commissioner Giles approaches Inspector Melville and warmly shakes his hand, "Well done. At least he is out of everyone's sight and mind during the election run-up. Hopefully, George Montague will vent his anger on Judge Menzies now, instead of me. You have done really well on this case. It has been a pleasure to work with you. I think you need a change from Downing Street. We need a new senior officer at Westminster station. Promotion to Chief Inspector. Yours if you want it."

"Thank you, Ma'am. I accept most gratefully."

"Excellent. I'll send you the paperwork. Our little secret for a few days. You need to return to Rochester Row. They're bringing Ms Du Bois there from the hospital."

"How is Sara Molan?"

"No change. Incidentally, Parliament has finally been dissolved but only after a rather brutal attack on the monarchy from you-know-who."

*

Melville has only been in the office at Westminster police station for a few minutes when a knock on the door is quickly followed by the entrance of a tall, slim woman, possibly in her mid to late twenties. Her jet-black hair falls over her shoulders and back. She is casually dressed in a T-shirt emblazoned with the words "Make A Difference. Smile" and tight jeans. She looks tired but even so is stunningly beautiful. "Inspector Melville, oui?"

"Oui," the Inspector replies. "You must be Ms Du Bois."

"Yes. Please call me Nic. Everyone else does."

"Please take a seat. I am sorry we must meet under these circumstances. How is Ms Molan?"

"Unconscious. I've been talking to her, but I just felt so stupid telling her what has been happening to me. Really, I've just spent three hours talking to myself."

"You never know. It might make all the difference. I know this is difficult for you, but I really need some information about Sara and anything she has told you in the last year or so."

"I'm fine. I just want to help in any way I can."

"Firstly, can I confirm your personal details please? Your full name?"

"Nicolette Madeleine Du Bois."

"Date of birth?"

"Twenty-first of August two thousand and five."

"Address?"

"Whilst I am in London, I plan to stay at Sara's

flat. I have keys and some of my stuff is still there. I would prefer not to give you my French address. It's complicated."

"OK. I have your phone number. That's fine. How did you meet Sara?"

"In a gay club. We just started talking and she bought me a drink. One thing led to another and I moved into her flat. We were together for three years and then that bastard Godwin messed up everything. I was working in Scotland and we rowed on the phone when Sara heard about the changes Godwin was planning. She panicked and that was that. I collected what I could carry when I went back to London. Sara was out and I've not seen her again until today."

"What work do you do?"

"Modelling. A bit of fashion but mostly glamour. Nude and topless. Am I shocking you, Inspector? I am not ashamed of my body but I'm twenty-eight years old now and there are so many beautiful twenty year olds now. My model days are numbered."

"Do you know anything about Sara's life before you met her?"

"She's Indian. She came to London when she was eighteen. She has family in India, but she never spoke about them. There was no contact at all when I was living with her."

"Did she ever talk about previous lovers?"

"There was someone in India before she left. She was doing the circuit until I met her."

"Doing the circuit?" queries Melville.

"Going around the clubs, picking up anyone you fancy. No commitment, just sex and move on to the next one."

"If Sara wanted privacy to the extent of keeping you a secret, why was she behaving like that?"

"She wasn't well known then. Just another want to be. She was single, attractive and sexually frustrated. I was the same back then. Once we found each other, that was it. No more clubbing. No more waking up with total strangers. Then she became well known and felt she must protect me from the press and the gossip."

"Did Sara ever pick up men?"

"Definitely not. She is one hundred per cent gay. She has no sexual interest in men at all. I'm bi but Sara is hardcore lesbian."

"When did you resume contact with Sara?"

"About a year ago. She rang me out of the blue to tell me that our relationship might be in the media. She wanted to know if I had talked to anyone. She sounded worried but said she was fine. It was probably going to blow away, but she wanted to warn me. I told her I had not spoken about her to anyone, and she was welcome to come to Marseilles if she needed to get away. She asked me if I thought we could get together again, and I told her I did not know but I would think about it. We spoke about three times more in the next few months. She always sounded worried, but she never told me why. Then, last evening, she rang to get me to ring Downing

Street. She said she was meeting the Prime Minister and he expected her to sleep with him. She was worried and needed an excuse to escape. She thought help would arrive before things got serious on Godwin's part. It must have happened more quickly than she expected."

"You must still have feelings for her to drop everything and fly to England."

"I love her. Always have. You do impossible things for someone you love." Nic pauses and wipes a tear from her left eye. "I am sorry. This is difficult for me."

"You're doing really well. Mr Godwin says he proposed to Sara last night. She turned him down because she still loves you."

"I hope that is true. There is just no way she would marry a man and especially not that man. She was frightened of him."

"Are you aware of anyone Sara may have dated since you left?"

"She wouldn't stay with me because she was so frightened of being caught in bed with another woman and jailed and flogged. I do not think she would take the risk."

"Godwin blackmailed Sara into that interview. He did not know she is gay. Do you have any idea what else he might be using against her?"

"Nothing. If it were me, I could give you a long list but not Sara. When we were together, her only interest was work. Climbing higher and higher."

"Godwin says that Sara drank three glasses of

champagne very quickly after the interview. Does that seem likely to you?"

"Sara drinks. So do I. When we were together, we drank everything from cheap cider to the best champagne."

"Would it have affected her judgement?"

"No. Sara is used to drinking. She might have got a bit sad but that is all."

"Nic, please do not be offended by this question. I must ask it because you will almost certainly be called as a witness at Godwin's trial. Is there anything in your life which the Prime Minister's legal team could use to discredit you?"

"When I broke up with Sara, I went to Paris. I had little money and work was hard to find. I had two or three men who gave me money to buy clothes or pay the rent. In return, I was their mistress when they did not want to go home. That is the French way. You have a wife at home, and you have a mistress at a different address. The two must never meet, of course."

"Were you seeing two or three at the same time?"

"Non. Certainement non. One at a time. I was a mistress not a prostitute."

"Anything else?"

"I had girlfriend in Lyons after I left Paris. She is in jail for stealing money from her employers. I was not involved. She always had money. I did not know where it came from. She went to prison. I went to Marseilles. I have not had sex in three years. I work when I can, and

I live quietly on my own. No scandal, no late nights, no, how do you say, honey daddies."

Melville laughs. "Sugar daddies. Well, you've certainly had your moments. I think you can expect to be questioned about your personal life. We cannot change it now, but prosecutors do not like surprises. If there is anything else at all, please tell me now."

"Rien. Nothing. I am not ashamed of anything I have done. I never steal or break law. In France, sex is essential part of day-to-day life. In England, for the last five years, sex is criminal offence. Nothing but boring intercourse between man and wife. No mistresses, no living together, no giving head and especially no homosexuality. You must all be crazy with passion and no means of relief. I have had many lovers, male and female and transgender, ever since I seduced my forty-five-year-old neighbour when I was fourteen but that is life, Inspector, not something to be ashamed of."

"I will ask an officer to drive you to Ms Molan's flat. Do you need to do any shopping?"

"I don't know what Sara has. Alcohol almost certainly but food I will need, I think."

Inspector Melville opens his wallet and hands Nic five twenty pound notes. "Take it please. Call it police expenses. There will be press and TV crews outside the flat. The officer will remove them, and I will arrange for a regular patrol of the area all night. Would you prefer a car outside?"

"Non. That is fine. As long as the officer goes in with

me. It will be very strange for me at first after five years."

"I'm going to ask the officer to look for anything about Sara's family, so they will definitely go in with you. I can organise an officer to stay overnight with you in the flat, if that would help."

"Are you offering?" Nic starts laughing, "Oh, you are blushing. You are bright red. How easy it is to embarrass les Anglais. It's alright. I am only kidding. Mind you, if you have a beautiful long-legged, busty blonde female constable available tonight, I could be interested."

"Right," says Melville nervously, "let's get you out of here before my blood pressure gets any higher."

After he sorts out Nic's ride to the flat, the Inspector returns to his office but is soon interrupted by Detective Constable Hellier. "Sir, we've had a message from the hospital about the victim. They say there are no signs of sexual activity or bruising to her genital area or her thighs."

"Thank you. That is interesting."

*

A few days later, Chief Inspector Melville receives a call from the Governor of Wandsworth prison, advising him that prisoner Godwin has been to see him, saying he wants an urgent meeting with Chief Inspector Melville. After consultation with Deputy Commissioner Giles, the meeting is arranged for the following afternoon.

CI Melville passes through security and is shown

into the empty visitor's room. Bob Godwin is brought in by two prison officers and takes a seat opposite the policeman. Melville is immediately shocked by the Prime Minister's appearance. He is walking stiffly and has difficulty in sitting down. Additionally, there is bruising on his face and his middle three teeth, top and bottom, are missing.

"It looks like you're having a rough time," begins CI Melville.

"This is a hellhole. They won't even talk about segregating me. I'm going to be dead in a week."

"I don't see what I can do to help. You need to speak to the Governor."

"Haven't they even told you why you're here?"

"I was told you wanted to see me. No more than that."

"This damn place. I want to do a deal with you. Move me out of here to a segregation unit. There must be one somewhere in the damn prison stock. All the prisons I built have them. I also want the rape charge dropped. Any sexual activity was definitely consensual."

"And what do I get?"

"Put me on trial this week. I'll plead guilty to attempted murder and you can go back to your day job. I want to be sentenced under the rules five years ago."

"That's not going to happen. Your Justice Act is still in force. You'll get flogged like everybody else sentenced at the moment."

"Come on, we all know it will be repealed as soon as

a new Government takes office. Then we'll have to wade through another trial to re-sentence me. I just want it all settled."

"I'm going to have to think about this."

"Don't take too long. I'm not going to survive much longer here."

Chief Inspector Melville phones Deputy Commissioner Giles from the prison and drives straight to a meeting with her.

After explaining Godwin's demands, he tells the Deputy Commissioner his views, "Without testimony from Sara Molan, the attempted rape charge is unsustainable anyway, so it seems reasonable to me to drop that one completely. With the attempted murder, we have a great case. There were only two people in a locked room. One is stabbed, the other is holding the murder weapon. Straightforward. On the other hand, we have two flaky witnesses with extremely questionable morals and enough secrets to keep any competent defence lawyer chomping at the bit for days. We ought to win but nothing is guaranteed. Being handed a guilty decision on a plate is too good to turn down. The problem arises with Godwin's demands. I am going to have to ask around for a segregation unit that has vacancies and can cope with a long-term guest. He is seeking sentencing under any system but his own. He wants imprisonment and nothing else."

"I agree with you about the attempted rape. I think we could easily lose the attempted murder. The defence will chew up the girlfriend and the boss and spit them out in little broken pieces. Let's get him into court urgently and get his guilty plea on record. I'll speak to Judge Menzies and see if he can help us wrap this up."

"Sentencing is the problem. Ideally, we need to wait until a new Government repeals the Justice Act. Will Menzies be willing to sentence under the previous legislation? I can't see him passing up the chance to flog the Prime Minister. If he agrees, what should we seek?"

"Menzies is a lot of things, but he is not a fool. He knows it is better to punish Godwin in some way rather than seeing him go free. I reckon fifteen to twenty years imprisonment. I imagine he will be out after half or even less. You're going to have to negotiate with Godwin. Try to keep above sixteen years if you can. I'll be happy at fifteen but nothing less. The defence and the judge will probably drive it down to fourteen anyway. Anything on the victim's family?"

"No, Ma'am. An officer has searched the flat but nothing at all referring to India. Not even an old Indian passport. Ms Du Bois will tell us if she comes across anything but for the time being any relatives will stay in blissful ignorance."

*

The next day, CI Melville is informed that Judge Menzies will hear the case in two days' time, so he returns to Wandsworth to speak to Godwin.

"We are agreeable to drop the attempted rape charge and we will, of course, accept your guilty plea to attempted murder. I have spoken to the Governor of Pentonville prison. They have a separate segregation unit of fifteen one-man cells. Normally, they are for short-term use but if you are prepared to stay for the length of your sentence then they are happy to keep you there for the entire duration of your punishment. It is self-contained and you will only leave your cell for exercise twice a day with no other prisoners around. In the circumstances, Judge Menzies is agreeable to sentence you under pre 2029 legislation. The prosecution has been told to ask for imprisonment for a period of between sixteen and twenty years. Your defence team can obviously ask for a different sentence and the judge will then reach a decision. Any questions?"

"I am representing myself. Surely you can come down on the prison term. I was thinking eight to ten."

"That's wildly optimistic but you can try. Ultimately, it is up to the judge. Everything else acceptable?"

"Yes. When can I go to Pentonville?"

"If everything goes perfectly at the trial, you will be taken directly from the court to the segregation unit. In two days' time, you will be as safe as you can possibly be. I'll see you in court."

*

The court hearing does not take up much of anyone's time. Bob Godwin pleads guilty to attempted murder and the prosecuting counsel withdraws the attempted rape charge. Judge Menzies asks each side to recommend a sentence. The prosecution requests sixteen to twenty years' imprisonment and the defendant suggests eight to ten years. The judge then announces his decision.

"This was a vicious attack on a young, vulnerable woman. It is to the defendant's immense credit that he has admitted the assault very early in the legal process. All parties have agreed that this defendant will be sentenced under punishment legislation in force prior to the Justice Act 2029. This is to speed up the sentencing protocol and avoid the necessity for re-sentencing when new legislation is passed following the forthcoming election. I need to consider the fact that Mr Godwin has been subject to severe retribution during his brief spell on remand. This has led to the regrettable situation where he needs to be kept apart from other prisoners, probably for the whole of his incarceration. Personally, I feel that some flogging and branding would be justified for the many people who have been subjected to barbaric violence in the last five years. Regrettably, this is not about me. I hereby sentence Robert Godwin to a term of imprisonment not exceeding twelve years. Please take the prisoner down and transport him to Pentonville prison forthwith, where I consider he will be safe and have a lot of time to consider the damage he has done to so many people during his term as Prime Minister."

*

Melville has only just entered Westminster police station after the sentencing when DC Hellier approaches him.

"Sorry, sir, but you may have to go straight out again. Ms Du Bois phoned. Ms Molan is starting to regain consciousness."

"No peace for the wicked, is there? If anyone wants me, I'll be at the Chelsea and Westminster."

Before entering Sara's hospital room, the CI asks the PC on guard what is happening.

"The victim is starting to come around. Not much more than a bit of eye opening and closing. Doc has been in and says it could be the first step towards full consciousness. Ms Du Bois is terribly excited and says Ms Molan spoke her name but the doctor thinks that is unlikely. Sir, what happened at court?"

"Twelve years. Not great but better than nothing. Let's hope Ms Du Bois sees it like that."

*

"*Twelve years. Twelve fucking years. Non. Non. C'est terrible.*"

As the PC outside hears this outburst, he smiles nervously and says to himself. "Guess she sees it differently to the Chief Inspector."

Inside the room, Nik bursts into tears and collapses into Chief Inspector Melville's arms. "It's alright," he says unconvincingly. "Cry it out. It's alright."

After a few minutes of sobbing and embarrassingly

soothing words normality, is restored.

"I am sorry. I never cry but this is all too much. You've let him get away with this."

"Nobody's got away with anything. Godwin has admitted attempted murder. He is nothing, just a common criminal. He will never be an MP again; nobody will ever trust him and when he comes out, there will still be many seeking revenge."

"I will be one of them."

"No, you won't be. You will be living happily ever after somewhere in deepest France with Sara. Now, what is happening here? She still looks unconscious to me."

"She keeps opening her eyes and looking around. She whispered 'Nic' to me once. The doctor thinks it will take several hours before she is conscious for more than a few seconds. I want to be here when she finally wakes up."

"We can phone you as soon as that happens. You look exhausted. I can get someone to take you home."

"Non. I stay as long as it takes. I was not there when she needed me, but I will be there this time."

Melville gently squeezes her hand and says, "There will be an officer outside if you want anything at all. Good luck."

Once outside the room, he sighs deeply and wonders what tomorrow will bring. In fact, there is a significant development even before the start of a new day. At ten PM, Sara Molan opens her eyes and starts talking. By the time CI Melville arrives at the hospital in the late morning, Nic is sitting on the edge of the bed holding Sara closely to her and the pair are conversing in French.

"My hero," shouts Nic and jumps up to embrace the Chief Inspector.

"Let him go. You're mine," Sara whispers hoarsely.

Melville disentangles himself from Ms Du Bois' clutches, which, in fact, proves more difficult than expected, and eventually manages to sit down beside the bed. "I'm Chief Inspector Melville and I am in charge of the investigation into your injuries. First of all, how are you?"

"So sore. I feel as if I've run full speed into a brick wall. So tired."

"Has Nic brought you up to date on what has happened whilst you've been unconscious?"

"No, she hasn't. She said you would do that."

"That was thoughtful of her." Those are the words that come out of his mouth but privately he wonders if there is a vacant isolation cell at Pentonville he can use after he has quietly strangled Nic. "I think that can wait until you are stronger."

"No. I want to know what that bastard did to me. Please."

"Alright but I stop at the first sign of distress. Agreed?"

Sara nods weakly.

"So, what is the last thing you remember?"

"Godwin saying to me that Nic was enjoying himself in Marseilles. I just flipped. He's spent a whole year threatening to expose my relationship with Nic. Saying he knows everything, and he would ruin me. Now he tells me Nic is male. I remember hitting him with my fists and swearing at him. After that, nothing."

"The police received a phone call from Nic just before nine o'clock and I went straight to the Prime Minister's rooms. When my officers and I reached the floor, you were screaming but then you stopped. Godwin wouldn't let us in, so we broke the door down. You were lying to the left of the door and bleeding heavily. Mr Godwin was standing by the food, holding the bloodstained carving knife. I asked Sergeant Adams to do what he could for you until the ambulance arrived. He had to do CPR on you."

"I would like to thank him."

"That can be arranged. I am not sure you would be talking to me now without his emergency first aid. I am trying to make sure he gets some kind of medal. One thing I do need to know is how we can contact your family or next of kin. They don't know that you have been hurt."

"I have no family. When I left India, I left my family there. Nic is my family, my next of kin now. Six years ago, I asked Nic to marry me, and she said yes. Today Nic has asked me to marry her, and I said yes."

"Well, congratulations to both of you."

"Is Godwin under arrest?"

"Better that that. He has admitted attempted murder and has already been sentenced to twelve years in jail. We felt unable to prosecute for attempted rape. He insists sex was consensual and, at best, it is your word against his. Now I have some details from you, I consider it doubtful your evidence would have helped, anyway. Godwin is in jail, in solitary confinement for his own protection. He has got intimately acquainted with some of his fellow prisoners and has had his front teeth knocked out. That is as good as we could manage."

"It is not as much as I would like, but he can do no harm in isolation. I would not have agreed to any form of intimacy with him or any other man, but I accept it is my muddled memory versus his word. Thank you for all you have done for Nic and myself."

"Sara, that's enough for now." He gestures to Nic to follow him outside. "What are your plans?"

"To look after her. It will take a long time to get the old Sara back, but we will get there. I think we will have to stay in London for a few months for treatment but eventually we will move to France and live happily ever after."

"I really hope you do. Despite Godwin's best efforts, we seem to have got the right result in the end."

"We are back to our situation five years ago. Life is good again. Thank you for everything. Au revoir."

"Au revoir, Nic," CI Melville exits quickly, before Ms Du Bois decides to hug him again.

CHAPTER 2

MONIQUE

June 2040

There are very few people on the beach in Calais despite the warm temperature and the sun blazing down from a cloudless sky. The few passers-by are all distracted by the topless beach babe stretched out on her back on a towel. Probably in her late twenties or early thirties, her long jet-black hair swept back over her shoulders, she possesses a stunning figure and a classic beauty more than sufficient to waylay beachcombers, although stopping traffic might be slightly beyond her nowadays. The thin, pale man lying alongside her attracts no attention whatsoever. He is approximately thirty years older than his companion, bald and looks in need of a decent meal and many more hours of sunshine. She is half asleep and oblivious to the occasional attention she is attracting. He alternates between reading from various pieces of paper in his hands and staring around him nervously.

About one o'clock, the woman wakes up, stretches and puts on her bikini top. She turns to her companion and says in English, "Time to start work, I think. We have a lot to do." The man doesn't answer but dutifully rearranges his papers and follows her across the beach road to an imposing two-storey villa. She opens the door and lets them both in. "I'm going to grab a shower. There's plenty to eat and drink in the fridge."

She re-emerges about ten minutes later wearing a skimpy, figure-hugging top and very tight shorts. She sits down beside the man on a sofa facing the sea. "Beautiful, isn't it?" she says in a strong French accent. "I am sorry to drag you across to the beach as soon as you arrived, but I think sunshine will help you relax. Shall we do the formalities first? I am Monique Trezequet. I am a freelance writer and I have been asked by your publisher to help write your life story. My understanding is that the publishers want, how do you say, a moles-and-all story."

The man laughs and says. "In England we usually say warts-and-all."

"Got it. They want a warts-and-all story. From your childhood right through to the present day. The publishers will cover all our expenses, but we will both only be paid when they have approved the completed book. I need the money and I would take a guess that you do as well, so let's be friends. We must work hard but I am sure we can play hard as well."

"Louise told me I would be working with a female writer, but she didn't mention how beautiful you were."

"Age and gravity are beginning to win these days."

"Not from where I am sitting."

"Now, behave yourself, Mr Godwin."

"Oh no. You must call me Bob. As long as I can call you Monique. Have you worked for Louise Land before?"

"Yes. I have helped some French entertainers write books, but I've never worked with anyone as important as you. Please be gentle with me because English is not my first language."

"I have no intention of being anything but extremely gentle with you." This remark from Bob Godwin is accompanied by a facial expression that can only be described as a leer. "I have only communicated with Louise Land by e-mail and text. What is she like?"

"A hard taskmaster. She expects perfection. She is totally trustworthy, and you won't find anyone with a bad word to say about her. She's built her publishing business up from nothing."

"Your English is very good. Where did you learn the language?"

"I lived and worked in London for a few years when I was much younger."

"Writing?"

"Non. I was modelling then. I got too old, so I turned to writing. A girl has to live, you know."

"You need a good man to look after you. Were you in London when I was Prime Minister?"

"No. I had moved back to Paris by then."

"Boyfriend?"

"Not at the moment."

"Tell me, how can someone so beautiful and sexy as you possibly be single."

"I am married to my work. What about you, Bob?"

"Well, as you know, I haven't been around women much in the last six years. I was married years ago but it didn't work out. Do you live in Calais?"

"No. I live in Paris. Louise thinks it is better for us to work here by the sea and where we are less likely to attract attention until we have finished the book."

"You were attracting plenty of attention earlier on, topless."

"Must be foreign tourists. The locals are used to topless women on the beaches. Perhaps I will sunbathe naked next time and really shock them."

"You'd probably be arrested for that in England."

"Such a repressed race."

"Not all of us, Monique. I assure you."

"Come on, enough of this talking. We have work to do."

"Must we? I'm very tired and I'd also like to explore Calais with you."

"Let's do a deal then. Two hours' work and then we'll look around. I have some money from Louise so perhaps we can go mad and have a meal and a drink or two. From tomorrow, it will be at least six hours' writing a day and my cooking, so make the most of it. Deal?"

"Yes, I guess so. I can see Louise isn't the only hard taskmaster around here."

They move across the room to a large desk and sit on either side. "How are we going to do this?" asks Bob.

"I want to work in order of events starting with childhood and finishing up with prison. Just talk to me. I will record everything, and we will edit it into a book when we've recorded everything. I will make some notes if something seems important and I may interrupt you to clarify something or if you go off track. Just talk to me normally and tell the truth. I'm starting the tape. Day one. Bob Godwin telling his life story to Monique Trezequet. Bob, can we start at the beginning please and talk about your family and childhood."

"I was born on the third of January 1978 in Derriford Hospital in Plymouth, Devon. My father, Brian Godwin, worked in the dockyards, had a violent temper and drank far too much," Bob pauses and speaks to his companion. "Monique, is this what you want?"

"Yes. You are doing brilliantly. Keep going."

"My mother. Eileen Godwin, nee Henderson, was ten years younger than my father. They got married when she was eighteen. She didn't work when I was really young but after I went to school she worked part-time on the till at the local Co-op."

"What is the local Co-op?" interrupts Monique.

"It was, and still is, a British supermarket chain. We lived in the Prince Rock area of Plymouth and they had a small shop close to where we lived. I am an only child, but there were plenty of other children around to play with. I went to Prince Rock Primary School when I was five. A couple of years after that, I began to take notice of what was happening around me. Dad often shouted at Mum and I, but when I was about seven, he started hitting me, either with his fists or his belt. One evening Mum tried to stand up for me and when he'd finished with me, he pushed her skirt up, pulled down her underwear and hit her again and again with his belt until she lost consciousness. I thought he'd killed her. That was the only time I saw him hit her, but I heard her crying at night many times. When I was nine, my mother started working late shifts at work. My father was either at the pub or drinking himself into oblivion in his chair. One night he ran out of beer, so he went to the Co-op to get some more. Mum wasn't there. As soon as she came home, they started arguing then she started screaming. I remember being really frightened. Eventually the noise stopped. The next morning, Mum woke me up early. She was black and blue all over her face. She told me that she was leaving my Dad and was going to live with somebody else. She said I had to stay with Dad until she and her new friend were settled then I could move in with them. I never saw or heard from her again. Someone told me years later that she moved away and had two more children with her new lover, who also worked at the Co-op. She didn't want me, so I never wanted her."

Bob's voice begins to break at this point, and he asks

Monique if he can have some water. Monique turns off the machine and goes into the kitchen, returning with a large jug of water and two glasses.

"I'm sorry. I didn't realise how difficult this would be for you."

"I'm alright. I haven't talked about any of this for so long. I am surprised it still hurts as much as it does. You can turn the machine back on. Dad ranted about her every night for years. I didn't really understand the words then but of course I soon did. Whore was one of his favourites. Adulteress. Jezebel. Floozy. Tart. I remember I got into trouble at school for calling a lady teacher a floozy. Dad drank more and more and worked less and less. Eventually he lost his job. That made him even more angry and he used to beat me up virtually every night. I started missing school because I didn't want the teachers to see my bruises. I moved from primary school to the local comprehensive, but I rarely went. Social services started coming round but I would hide in my bedroom and my father would tell them I had gone off to school that morning. Just after my thirteenth birthday, a woman called round from the school. Dad fed her the normal story but this one insisted on looking around. I hid in a wardrobe in my bedroom. Unfortunately, my uniform was flung across my bed and it did not take her long to discover my hiding place. I got taken into care and spent the next three years drifting between foster homes and council facilities. At least I usually got fed and went to school every day. I left school for good at sixteen. I saw my father once in those three years when we both happened to be on the same bus. He looked awful, kept coughing and bringing up stuff. He died when I was eighteen. I was the only one at his funeral."

"That's enough, Bob. If you don't need a drink, I do. Let's get dressed up and hit the town. We'll start tomorrow with you leaving school and looking for work."

Whilst Bob settles for a conventional jeans and jacket combination, Monique dresses herself in an ankle length white dress split up the right thigh and cut low enough at the top to make sure her leg doesn't get all the attention. The meal goes well, the drinking even more so. It is two very merry revellers who arrive back at the villa shortly after midnight.

"Let's have one more drink," says Bob, enthusiastically.

"Non. I have to report to Louise. You stay up and have as many as you like. Early start tomorrow and we need to make real progress. Goodnight. Oh, and by the way, my door will be locked when you come up and I have the only key so don't waste your time trying to break in," responds Monique as she leaves the room.

A few minutes later, with the door locked, Monique speaks to Louise in Paris. "He arrived safely. We've started the recording. We're going to do his childhood and early career briefly and then move on to the more important stuff in greater detail."

"Any problems so far?"

"A few suggestive comments and the odd wandering hand in the restaurant but I expected that. He got a bit upset talking about his parents. His mother walked out on him and her husband to live with another man."

"An adulteress in the family, then."

"Yes. It's all a bit depressing at the moment."

"Do you need anything from me?"

"No, we're fine. I'm taking him over to the beach whilst the cleaner tidies the place up. Today was a quiet start. I'm going to make him suffer from now on." They both laugh before Monique continues, "I'll ring you tomorrow night. Au revoir."

"Au revoir. Don't work him too hard."

The routine is the same the next day, although Monique carries out her threat to sunbathe naked. She does, however, spare the blushes of locals and tourists to some extent by lying on her front. Bob Godwin refuses point blank to join her au naturel and spends the time reading his papers yet again and leering unseen at his companion. After a couple of hours on the beach, they return to the tidy, clean villa and soon commence work.

Monique sets up the taping equipment, opens her notebook and says, "The tape is on. This is day two. We will start from your father's funeral and go on to your working life and your marriage."

"Well, at sixteen, I sort of fell out of the care system and I also left school with no qualifications. I found work at a used car lot. Started by making tea and cleaning the cars twice a day. I may have flopped out of school, but I am not totally thick. I watched the salesmen, the bad ones more than the good ones at first. Once I felt that I knew where the poor sellers were making their mistakes, I started to concentrate on how the good ones did it. I waited for my chance and one day, when a couple of the reps were off sick, I asked if I could have a go. Sold a car that had been on the lot for weeks at the selling price first time out. Somebody else made the tea and cleaned the cars after that. I was sometimes living with Dad, but mostly sleeping on sofas. I had a mate called Tim Robbins and I stayed with him a lot. There was a girl a year older than me living opposite who I knew slightly from school. Her name was Christine Taylor. I asked her out a couple of times, but she said no. Anyway, Tim was seeing a girl named Anne and she had a friend called Diane, so they set up a date for me with this Diane. Christine saw us together and got jealous, so after a day or two she said she would go out with me. I remember Tim got annoyed I'd dumped Diane and threw me out. He did forgive me in the end. Anyway, Christine and I became an item. For a time, at least. Over the next couple of years, we split up five times and got back together every time."

"What were the reasons for the splits?" asks Monique.

Bob answers immediately, "Sex, basically. It was the nineties. AIDS had happened so everyone was trying to practice safe sex. Marriage was beginning to lose popularity and in my little world most of the people I knew were living together. Christine wanted to wait until we were married. I wanted to consummate the deal as quickly as possible. Money was another factor, and I don't think her father liked me very much either. Then my father died, as I mentioned earlier. He rented our house, so I had nowhere to live. However, he did have an insurance policy on his life. Paid in a quid a week for years. I was the beneficiary and suddenly I had money. Work was going really well, and I rented a one-bedroomed flat. I did suggest to Christine that she move in with me, but I can recall her response to this day, 'Not without a wedding ring, Bob Godwin.' This went on for a year or so. In the end, I blinked first and we got married in September 1997. I was nineteen, she was twenty. We loved each other but we were young, inexperienced in life and clueless about sex." Bob pauses and sighs before continuing.

"At least work was going great. I was outselling everyone else at work and Christine got a job in a call centre. We decided to wait to have children. Marriage was thrilling for about six months, then alright for about another six months and then hell on earth for the next five years. I lost track of how many times she went home to her parents. Usually, she came back in a few days but one time she was away for about ten weeks. When we were together, we argued nonstop about anything and everything. What we were going to eat, some remark her mother had made and, of course, sex. Don't forget the only experience of marriage I had was my parents. One night we had a real humdinger of a row and she threw a plate at me. I grabbed her, yanked down her trousers and underwear and put her across my knee. I spanked her bare backside until it was scarlet, and my hand was so sore I simply couldn't hit her anymore. She went back to her parents, but she came back eventually after I promised not to hit her again."

"Did you?"

"Yes, I did. I never punched her, but I punished her with my hand or a cane."

"Why?"

"Because she deserved it. By the time we got to our sixth wedding anniversary, we were only communicating through beatings, screams and swear words. She left me and never came back. We mutually agreed to divorce and that was that. She married again a couple of years after the divorce and moved away. I lost touch. I thought she might come out of the woodwork when I became well known but she didn't."

"How do you feel about her now? Do you regret punishing her so badly?"

"I feel sad that we couldn't make it work. I did love her, but we were both too young. Marriage was supposed to be this wonderful fairy-tale life where you all lived happily ever after. Nobody told us it was hard work. I said before that the only example of married life I had was my parents. Rows and violence. My father viewed my mother as his possession, and I suppose I felt the same about Christine. Nowadays I imagine the experts would say I was abusing her. I didn't think that at the time. Marriages need discipline. The man is the head of the family. We have been on the slippery slope to disaster ever since all this equality nonsense. Standards have been allowed to fall and the old order has been sent packing. But there is nothing replacing it except protests, contempt for authority and a total lack of discipline. The youth of today think about nobody but themselves. Not their families, their employers or their neighbours. *It's just me first and everybody else can fuck off. A good spanking or thrashing never hurt anyone.*"

Bob pauses at this point to compose himself. Monique looks shocked but chooses to say nothing and waits patiently for Mr Godwin to calm down.

"I'm sorry about that, Monique. I have very strong views on standards and discipline. It wasn't all one way in my marriage. Christine's plate throwing improved over time. I had to go to A&E twice for stitches. Anyway, Christine left me, and I concentrated on my work. About three years later, my boss said he was thinking of retiring in a year or two and would I be interested in buying half the business now and the rest when he finished completely. It would give me a chance to learn from him before being left on my own. So, I went to a bank and got a loan. I paid it off one month and then took out another loan the next month because he decided I was doing fine on my own and packed it all in. The business boomed under my control. We expanded into other cities and I became well off. The wealthier I became, the luckier I got with women.

Times were changing. Marriage was considered old hat. Living together as partners was suddenly the only way to have a relationship. I met a woman called Danielle and we were together for a couple of years until she fell for another woman, would you believe? That hurt me very badly. It is not right for a woman to replace her man with another woman. Unnatural. But that is the twenty-first century for you. People will be allowed to marry their pets next, I expect. Do you take Rover to be your lawful wedded husband and to ensure he always has enough bones, and that you honour his health by taking him to the vets regularly?"

Monique interrupts quickly before Bob starts ranting again, "I think that's enough for this morning. Time for lunch and a nice break before we carry on this afternoon. That is great. I think I will refer back to some of the things you've said today when we move on to your political career. Come on, let's eat."

Over lunch, Monique tries to soothe Bob by talking about safe topics such as golf, London, Paris and clothes. The discussion on the last subject is completely one-sided, of course, with Bob showing little interest in Monique's views on what is in and what is out this year. However, both are more relaxed when they resume work.

"There was little change over the next few years. I had the odd date, but nothing felt quite right. Business boomed. I made a lot of money and I spent most of it. I built a huge mansion and drove the finest cars.

My cooking is inedible at best, so I ate out at the best restaurants in Devon and Cornwall. Then, in 2020, I met Lucy. I had advertised for a secretary and Lucy applied. She came in for an interview and I was in love before she even sat down. She had a bubbly personality, short blonde hair, a great figure and was wearing a short, but not too short, skirt. I was forty-two years old; she was twenty. It took about two minutes to realise she had no idea at all about being a secretary and I told her on the spot she wouldn't be getting the job, but would she like to go to lunch with me? After lunch, we went back to my mansion and spent the afternoon in bed. The only time in my life I got a fuck on the first date. Lucy moved in and I proposed after six weeks. It was perfect. Work was difficult and the country was in and out of lockdowns due to the pandemic. I had to furlough a lot of staff."

"What is furlough?" Monique interrupts.

"Laying off staff but keeping them on the books. The Government paid part of their wages and when things improved the staff were still available to come back and work for me again. I think some other countries had similar schemes. It worked very well but overall Covid was a disaster for me. I had to sell online, which is not easy with second-hand cars. People want to see used cars, touch them and drive them. I guess I spent too much time working, often late at night. But Lucy never complained. Sex was incredible. I think it is best if I just say she taught me things I never knew could be done between two consenting adults. We planned to marry but the restrictions due to the pandemic went on and on. By mid-2021, all my yards were open again and doing well. Social events were happening again, and I was invited to a dinner at my golf club. Lucy didn't want to go. When we were mingling at the bar after the meal, an old friend, a policeman, took me into another room. He told me that a friend of his had said that he had seen Lucy in Union Street touting for business. He told me I must never reveal his name because he had done some checking, illegally, in police records and found she had three convictions for prostitution in London and Guildford. She also had one conviction for robbing a client. I finished my drink in one swallow and drove straight down to the red-light district of Plymouth. By chance I was driving one of the pool cars from work that day, so she didn't recognise me when I stopped alongside her. I pulled down the passenger window and she came over. She turned white when she saw me. I just said, "Get in." I drove her home and told her to get her stuff. I told her to go and never come back. Then I drank until I passed out. I loved her so much. If she had been shagging another bloke, I would probably have forgiven her but not prostitution. Walking around Union Street half dressed, performing sick acts in the back of cars, risking her sexual health as well as mine. I heard on the grapevine that she left Plymouth, but I have no idea where she went or what she has got up to. I guess there is no fool like an old fool."

Bob stops at this point and appears to be lost in his

thoughts. Monique, to her great surprise, feels sympathy for him. She walks around the desk and puts her arm on his shoulder. He asks her, "Why did she do it? She could have everything she wanted. I thought we had a great sex life. Why did she want sleazy encounters in car seats or back alleys with total strangers?"

Monique hugs him and replies hesitantly, "I don't know. Some do it to buy drugs or feed their children. I suppose some do it because they love sex or are addicted to the thrill of doing something naughty in public with a complete stranger. I get a kick out of sunbathing topless or nude. I know it is risky. I might be raped or reported to the police, but I still do it. People do stupid things sometimes. You are not responsible for Lucy's actions any more than you are responsible for mine."

Bob turns round in his chair. There are tears in his eyes.

"Thank you," he says quietly. "I'm fine. Let's go on. Anyway, that was 2021. The following year, a guy rang me out of the blue. He said he owned used car lots in the Midlands and wanted to expand into the South West. He wondered if I was interested in selling up as it would be cheaper to take over an existing chain than to start from scratch. I had him checked out and he was squeaky clean, so we talked money. I made him promise not to get rid of any of my staff for at least a year and I took his money. I was effectively retired at forty-four. So, there I was. Forty-four years old, loaded, living in luxury and very single. Playing golf, dining out and watching daytime television soon lose their attraction when you are doing them every day. One morning, I saw David McDougall on a political programme talking about his vision of reducing crime and handing out tough sentences to anyone convicted by a court. I was enthralled. I contacted David and eventually we founded the Common Sense Party. At first it was just something to do but I got deeper and deeper into it. A few people backed us financially and a year before the 2029 election we were able to fight every parliamentary seat. We had a wonderful manifesto and all we had to do was work hard on promoting the party. David was the face of Common Sense, but I worked my fingers to the bone behind the scenes. About a month before the election, one of the backers told me that the Executive Committee wanted me to be leader of the party in Westminster, providing I was elected."

"Do you know why you were chosen?"

"No idea. There were some important people behind the scenes. It was well known that I thought David was too much of a moderate. When I was approached, the party was doing well in the polls and some kind of presence in the House of Commons was looking quite likely. I imagine they thought I would cope better with the pressures than David. He is a great communicator but, as he proved, he didn't have the backbone or the stomach to fight in support of the party's policies or press on through criticism. Anyway, when the results started coming in on election night, it soon became clear that we were winning, and people started calling me Prime Minister and congratulating me. David was nowhere to be seen. It just seemed like a dream. I think I only realised it was real when I was bundled into a limousine and taken to Buckingham Palace to meet King Charles and offered the chance to form a Government."

"Bob, that's great. We'll stop now and move on to your years in power tomorrow. I reckon it will take us several days to go through all that. I'm sorry some of today's subjects proved so upsetting for you."

"It is hard to relive bad times. You think you have come to terms with the past, but it can still wound you decades later. Monique, I really need a hug."

They both rise from their chairs, meet in the middle of the room and embrace. It is Monique who takes the initiative and starts kissing Bob passionately. She then takes him by the hand and leads him up to her bedroom. Nothing is said as she unbuttons his shirt and starts rubbing her hand across his bare chest. They pull apart just long enough to take all their clothes off and then continue the kissing and fondling. It is Bob's turn to make the next move as he guides Monique to her bed and then gently positions himself on top of her. The silence is soon broken by moans from Monique as Bob enters her slowly and begins thrusting to and fro, slowly to begin with and then faster and faster. At the same time, he begins to use both hands to softly stroke her magnificent breasts and squeeze her erect nipples. Monique responds with low moans of pleasure which turn to louder and louder groans as the thrusting increases and the touching continues. He leans forward to kiss her on the lips, and she repositions herself slightly so he can edge his head downwards to caress her neck and then her breasts. The thrusting into her vagina becomes frantic. She moans loudly, then lets out a triumphant scream as she feels a warm wetness inside her.

*

A few hours later, Monique creeps out of her bedroom, leaving Bob asleep and rings Louise Land, "Hi, it's me."

"How are you getting on?"

"Fine. We're up to the election. It's going to be slower progress now because you want an in-depth look at everything that happened whilst he was Prime Minister, including the attack, don't you?"

"Yes, I do. Unless you have problems with him, I don't think I'll come down until you've almost finished the whole thing. Are you keeping him sweet?"

"He gets very emotional remembering his past and his lost loves. Some feminine attention is required from time to time."

"Have you fucked him yet?"

Monique hesitates before replying, "Would it be a problem if I had?"

"I take it that means you have. And the answer to your question is no. I don't want him walking away. We've both got too much invested in this. Do whatever is necessary to keep him there until I arrive. I almost forgot; I've sent you some photographs you may find useful. I've sent them to Avelle's address. She'll leave the unopened envelope for you whilst she's cleaning tomorrow".

"That's great. I'm trying to avoid her if at all possible. The less she sees of us, the better. I'll speak tomorrow. I think it will be a difficult day. I've let him have a pretty easy ride so far, because it doesn't really matter if he's telling the truth about his past life or not."

"Sleep well."

Monique goes back into the bedroom and cuddles up against her new lover. Bob stirs slightly but does not wake up. She settles down and wonders when she will be back in the arms of her true love.

*

The next morning, Monique is up and doing exercises in tracksuit bottoms and a sweat-stained T-shirt in the main room downstairs when Bob joins her.

"I prefer you naked," he says cheerfully.

"Do you?" she asks. "Well, you know the routine. Breakfast, beach, then work. Then I'll see what I can do – later, much later. Can you go to your own room and make the bed look as if it's been slept in? I don't want the cleaner to know about anything we get up to in here, business or pleasure."

"Certainly, beautiful. Anything to please," Bob says as he exits the room to go back upstairs.

To his surprise, Monique keeps on her exercise clothes to go to the beach. The reason soon becomes clear. "No lazing about today. We are going jogging. Just to the other end of the beach and back."

"What's with the 'we'? I promise you I will still be here when you come back," Bob replies, trying to hide his anxiety.

"No jogging this morning equals separate rooms tonight."

Bob is soon lagging behind his super-fit companion. He's about three quarters of the way out towards the end of the beach when Monique passes him heading back. Fighting the temptation to cheat and tag on behind her, he struggles on to the far end and then plods back to the starting point and Monique. "Don't do that to me again," he says, breathlessly.

Monique laughs but doesn't answer. She has removed her running clothes and is lying on her back rather incongruously wearing bikini bottoms and an unattractive black sports bra.

"What on earth is that?" he asks, trying not to laugh.

"This is a form of torture you men know nothing about. At least it stops me having two black eyes. Help me take it off." Bob is only too willing to assist as it means he can once more gaze upon her voluptuous breasts.

All too soon, they are back at the villa. A large brown envelope is sitting on the kitchen table and, out of sight of her companion, Monique places it in a drawer.

A few minutes later, they are back seated in their

usual positions and starting work on the third day of their project.

Monique says, when they are ready to start, "We're on to your period as Prime Minister now and I want to do things differently. It is going to be very boring for us and the readers to go through everything in fine detail. So, what I propose is that I ask you to talk about specific subjects in as much detail as possible. Does that sound feasible?"

"I don't see any problems. Let's see how we get on," replies Bob.

"Great. The tape is on. Can we talk about your first few days as Prime Minister?"

"The main thing I remember is being rushed from place to place by loads of people I didn't know. I went straight from Buckingham Palace to Downing Street to meet the staff and then on to a television studio to be interviewed by Sara Molan. I had never seen or heard of her before as David McDougall had handled all the media stuff. At the time it all felt like a whirl, but I think it went very well and, of course, there was an instant connection between the two of us. Sara said towards the end about future interviews and all I could think was I don't want to do this ever again. I didn't think, I just said no more interviews, but I might consider doing one or two with Sara and I would issue details of what was happening in Government. That was a masterstroke because I could concentrate on the important stuff and feed information to the press when I wanted to instead of facing daily interruptions, like Boris Johnson during the pandemic. The press meetings were a total waste of time, saying the same thing conference after conference and then being asked questions he had already answered. I could control what the media and the public knew and get someone else to read out the pronouncements. On that first day, I chose my cabinet. I had a list of the Common Sense MPs and some brief details of their backgrounds. I only knew about four of them personally, so it was a case of trying to match them as best I could. They all survived the whole five years, so I reckon I did a good job on that. No need for time-wasting cabinet reshuffles if you do it right at the start."

"What about David McDougall?"

"David's background was in television and reporting on politics. How on earth did he expect to run the economy or handle foreign affairs? With hindsight, I suppose I should have given him something. Later on, I founded a Ministry of Decency to preserve standards in the media. That did not really do the job I wanted it to do. David would have made a good head of that because he understood broadcasting and what you should say and what you should never say. Unfortunately, he was an independent MP by then. As soon as I had the right people in the right jobs, I worked my way through the various Heads of State who wanted to talk to me and then I began to formulate the policies needed to make the nation great again. Over the next few days, I reorganised my personal staff and tightened up security inside and outside Downing Street. It is a great irony that I authorised the transfer to Downing Street of Paul Melville, who handled the investigation into Sara's stabbing. Going back to David, he did not take kindly to being left out of my ministerial choices and said some unhelpful things about the party and myself. He refused to stop sniping at his own side, so he decided to go out on his own."

"David McDougall is on record as saying he was sacked from the party."

"If he was then that was down to the Executive Committee. They ran the party. I ran the country."

"Who were the members of this mysterious Executive Committee?"

"I do not feel able to divulge that information. They were made up of supporters of the party. Very important people who would not thank me for naming them, even after six years."

"Let us move on then to the Justice Act 2029. Who wrote it and why was it so much more severe than the election manifesto?"

"I think the reason David was not chosen to lead the party was that he was considered too moderate. He contributed to the manifesto which, for instance, stated that the death penalty would be re-introduced for all murderers. David kept trying to water that down with various exceptions and wanted the party to use a humane method of execution, whatever that might be. I was known to be in favour of a stronger approach. As an example, I do not believe in showing murderers the slightest humanity. They are cold-hearted killers and, unfortunately, the rest of society have to be equally cold-hearted in how we deal with them. Many clauses of the Act matched the manifesto completely. I would liken the manifesto to a rough plan. The legislation is the finished product, definitely more detailed and hopefully massively improved as well."

Monique butts in at this point. "Homosexuality, for example. There is no mention of making this a criminal offence in the manifesto. Then along comes the Act and every step forward the gay community had made in decades is lost overnight. Whose idea was it to criminalise same-sex relationships?"

"Mine. It was a subject that nobody mentioned in manifesto discussions. I consider homosexuals to be immoral. The human race would die out if it were left to them. I do not understand how a human being can be attracted to their own sex. The mere thought of doing it with another man makes me feel sick. I've been in prison, remember. It's beyond disgusting. I chose to spend six years in isolation rather than have another minute with those animals. The Bible says sex is only to take place between a man and his wife. Homosexuals are wrong in every way. Anyhow I put a spike in their wheels, didn't I?"

"The world is supposed to be a kind place. Tremendous progress had been made in allowing everybody to live equally regardless of their skin colour, their gender or whoever they choose to fall in love with. Who are you to say what other people do in the privacy of their own homes?"

"Are you going to complain about my increasing sentences for interfering with children? Of course not, because youngsters need to be protected from themselves because they are inexperienced in the ways of the world. The adults who prey on them are scum with no respect for anyone or anything but their perversion."

Monique fights to control her temper and tries hard to pick her words carefully in her reply, "They are two completely different things. Obviously, I do not want children to be sexually abused and taken advantage of because they are naïve and vulnerable. That is why many countries have an age of consent to ensure legal protection. Fully grown adults do not need Government protection or interference in their personal lives. This is the twenty-first century. We've all evolved since the cavemen. Just because something isn't to your taste does not give you the right to ruin people's lives. You are so keen on preventing children from abuse, but you have no qualms about beating your wife until her ass resembles a traffic light. That is fine, isn't it? It's not abuse though, because you are teaching her, so she won't make the same mistake again. Doing her a favour really because she's just a stupid woman. Are homosexuals supposed to be grateful to you for taking the time out to beat, brand and imprison them so they will know better next time?"

"The answer is yes. When I was Prime Minister, they were doing something illegal and immoral. Child, adult or animal, they all need to be taught when they do something wrong. The stick is always better than the carrot. You are entitled to your views, but I do not like being spoken to in that tone. I won't let it pass a second time."

"*Are you threatening me?*" asks Monique, incredulously.

"No, just warning you. I do not take kindly to being lectured by a woman over twenty years my junior."

"Time for lunch, I think," says Monique, rising. She is halfway to the kitchen before the last word reaches Bob's ears. Once in a different room to Bob, she retrieves the envelope and opens it. She looks at the photographs contained inside and looks at each in turn before rearranging the order and replacing them all in the envelope.

Lunch is eaten in silence, which is probably a good thing. Too soon they are back at the desk for the afternoon session with the envelope now on the floor beside Monique.

"Why did you decide to ban all heterosexual relations between unmarried couples?"

"To maintain standards and take a firm stand against promiscuity. Marriage provides security as well as morality. Children need to be brought up in a stable, legal relationship."

"I would like to talk about Leanne Hervey." Monique picks up the envelope and takes out the top photograph, which she puts face up on the desk. "Leanne was sixteen when you came into power. She was living with her boyfriend at her parents' house. The police raided the house, caught them in bed together and arrested them. Leanne admitted that the sexual relationship had started when she was aged fifteen. She was sent to youth detention, savagely beaten and branded. When I look at that picture, I see a beautiful teenage girl with her life in front of her, ruined by the four letters burnt into her forehead. 'S-L-U-T'. Is that how you protect children from older men? What do you see when you look at her?"

"I see a sinner. I see a criminal who is very unlikely to offend again. Thanks to Sir Keir Starmer, who replaced me as Prime Minister, she can cover the branding up these days."

Monique puts another picture down on the desk. This shows a young man showing vivid scars on his bare back. The marks crisscross from his shoulders down to his waist. Some of the wounds are clearly bleeding.

"This is Liam, Leanne's boyfriend. The photograph was taken by a prison doctor three days after Liam received two hundred and fifty strokes of the cat. The scars continue down to the back of his knees. You cannot see the branding of 'Paedophile' on his forehead. He was seventeen when that picture was taken."

"Criminals were punished severely. So what? If you don't break the law, you don't get punished. There has to be law and order. There must be discipline. Don't waste your time showing me any more of your precious photos. You are not going to change my mind. They are criminals and they deserved everything they got."

"Okay. It's not only me you need to convince but also everyone who reads the book. I would like to talk about the death penalty for all murderers."

"This was mentioned in our manifesto and warmly welcomed by voters up and down the country."

"Nothing was said about the execution method, though."

"I accept that, and I also accept that David McDougall was going around the country telling voters the death sentence would be carried out humanely. There isn't a nice way of killing anyone and if there was, I'd be damned if I would use it on murderers. David McDougall got his knickers in a twist about Aaron Davis, some half-wit who murdered a shopkeeper. There was a protocol to protect anyone with genuine mental problems but that did not apply in this case. I offered Sara Molan an exclusive interview if she gave David a hard time. She chose to be a good girl for once and David stormed out of the studio. The protests petered out after that for some reason."

"Was it really necessary for Aaron to be stripped naked and ripped to pieces by a firing squad on live television?"

"An important part of any punishment is the deterrent value to others. For any deterrent to be successful, it must be nasty and visible. Nobody will be prevented from committing murder by seeing a killer tucking into a splendid meal and then just a few words on the news that an execution has taken place. The murder rate dropped by ninety per cent during my term in office. Six years on, it is higher than before I was elected. So many innocent lives lost. So many guilty lives spared. Don't ask me to apologise for any aspect of the death sentence when I was Prime Minister. It was wanted by the public. It was needed. It worked. The liberals and do-gooders hated it, which, to me, means that it must be the right thing to do if they are against it."

"I was wondering if anyone in your circle was murdered?"

"No. Why do you ask?"

"Well, your mother committed adultery, so you made it a criminal offence and made sure offenders received horrific punishment. Your next serious relationship ended when your girlfriend left you for another woman and the entire gay community paid in blood and ruined lives for that. Then your fiancée had a sideline as a prostitute, and you persecuted her successors with admirable vigour. I just wondered if you had a personal reason for going after murderers. Apparently not, just cold-blooded butchery."

The reaction from Bob is immediate. He rises and is around the table before Monique can react. He grabs her and drags her off her chair. "I warned you," he screams at her. He pushes her onto the floor and pulls the electric flex out of the tape recorder. Standing over her, he orders, "*Get undressed, now.*" Monique makes no response and receives two painful blows with the flex across her legs. "Now!" Bob yells. Fighting back tears, Monique begins to undress. "You were warned. You have to learn discipline and respect."

Monique is soon clothed only in bra and panties. "Everything off," Bob snaps and she is soon stark naked. "Lie face down on the sofa." Whilst she is doing this, he closes the curtains. He raises the flex and brings it down on her buttocks. For a second, Monique feels nothing, then a burning pain reaches her senses, and she screams. Almost immediately, a second stroke comes and then a third. Her verbal protests are soon joined by tears pouring down her face, but the lashing continues. Soon her entire back and her thighs are on fire as well as her buttocks. The blows keep coming. At last, there is a pause. "Turn over on to your back." She does so but with great difficulty and pain. "Now, hold still. I don't want to hit your face." Through her tears, Monique can only watch in horror as the vicious flex bites into her breasts again and again, adding each time to her agony. Finally, it is all over. She rises stiffly from the sofa, still crying uncontrollably. "Go and rest in bed," Bob orders. "I'll join you later."

That remark is the final straw for Monique, "*No, you fucking won't. You don't get to beat the crap out of me one minute and fuck my brains out the next. You're sleeping on your own from now on, Mister.*"

She moves painfully over to her clothes, picks them up with great difficulty and hobbles upstairs, locking her bedroom door behind her. She finds it impossible to get comfortable, although there is a slight reduction in pain after about half an hour. Once Monique is sure she has heard Bob come to bed, she rings Louise Land.

"Hello," she says, before bursting into tears.

"Monique, what on earth has happened?"

"I'm all right, really. Sorry. I thought I'd finished crying."

"Take your time. Just tell me what is wrong."

"I've been punished so I will know better than to challenge him next time. He's hit me front and back with an electric cable flex. Louise, it's not abuse, apparently, because like a child or an animal I have to be taught respect and the right way to behave."

"Have you got anything to put on the wounds?"

"I've got some soft cream I'll put on when the pain subsides a bit."

"You need to get out of there before he kills you."

"He won't kill me unless it's through boredom at hearing him rant on and on. No, I'm not giving up now. Today's work ended early for obvious reasons, so I reckon I'm going to need all of tomorrow and most of the day after to cover the rest of his Prime Ministership, his meeting with Sara Molan and the prison years. So, I suggest you come down late afternoon or early evening the day after tomorrow. I'll get everything together before you arrive."

"I'm not happy about this. I'll never forgive myself if anything happens to you."

"Let's not be forced into doing things differently just because he's a sadist. We're too close now to risk throwing it all away. He's been determined to stop me sunbathing nude. Looks like he's managed it this time. Honestly, I'll be fine. See you in about forty-eight hours."

"Are you absolutely sure?"

"Positive. Goodnight."

*

It proves to be a long night for Monique. Every time she manages to fall asleep, the pain soon wakes her again. She abandons any further attempt to sleep at five AM and takes stock of her situation. Her breasts are bruised rather than cut and are less sore than the night before. "No bra today, then" she mutters to herself. The rear view shows that she is covered in cuts, welts and streaks of blood from her shoulders to her thighs. Using the mirrors, she can take photos with her phone of her injuries. One consolation is that she can move more easily, as much of yesterday's stiffness has eased. She roots through her clothing and finds a silk blouse and a long, soft white skirt. She checks they are not too see-through and puts them on without any underwear. She gets downstairs without too much trouble but soon finds she needs a cushion to be able to sit for any length of time. She is just finishing getting breakfast ready when Bob comes downstairs. They sit together in silence for a few minutes before Monique speaks.

"I spoke to Louise last night. She wants me to get out before you turn violent again. I have told her I'm staying to finish what I have started. But I want you to listen to me. I am not stupid. If I think I am in any danger at all, I will be out of here before you can say 'Strip.' And if I go, your payment for doing this book goes with me. I hate you and you hate me but, hopefully, we can unite over our financial needs. We both need to get this finished so are you going to leave the electric cables alone?"

"Have you learnt to behave respectfully?"

"Yes, but that doesn't mean I'm not going to challenge you on certain matters. That's my job and I will not be frightened into not doing it at all or letting you get away with some ridiculous statement unchallenged. Now, can we see this through?"

"Yes. I'll say one thing for you. You've got guts, I'll give you that."

"I suggest after breakfast we get a taxi and go into the centre. I'm not really into sunbathing or walking too far today, for some reason."

The shopping trip produces two extra soft cushions, several litres of soothing creams and a thong.

Back in the villa, with Monique sitting on three cushions, they get back to the Justice Act 2029.

"Can we start with reintroducing the cane into schools? Do you think that was successful?"

"Honestly, I would say yes and no. It was very well supported during the election campaign and something that was desperately needed to reduce truancy levels and promote learning. I think there were problems because, with hindsight, we should have set a maximum number of strokes based either on age or offence. The cases that hit the headlines, like Leah Stafford and Warren, were rare examples where the punishment was excessive. Unfortunately, do-gooders like David McDougall and Sara Molan blew things out of all proportion. The decision to allow employers to punish employees was much more successful for two reasons. Firstly, the employee could choose whether to involve the police and the courts or accept punishment from the employer. Secondly, bosses seemed to have a more realistic approach to punishment. Ninety-nine per cent of employees facing punishment chose not to go to court. I am not aware of any major unhappiness amongst those who accepted their fate within their workplace. The idea was to have a system of corporal punishment that started at school backed up by parental action, leading on to the workplace or further education. Of course, anyone breaking the law would be dealt with by the courts and their sentencing methods. A child would be caned at school and then subjected to corporal punishment throughout their adult working life. There was far less co-operation from parents than I expected which is why I gave schools consent to proceed against parents' wishes. That, regrettably, made matters worse with parents claiming their views were being ignored by cane-happy teachers."

"You seem now to accept that some children were

subjected to overly zealous punishment. At the time you defended the system and the level of punishment extremely forcibly, primarily in your interview with Sara Molan."

"Yes, I did. That was a difficult interview. I expected Sara to support me, but she decided to follow her own agenda. I believed very strongly that we needed to enforce discipline in schools, in the home and in the workplace to improve behaviour and efficiency in every single citizen. It was working. Crime was down. Schools became places where children could learn in a safe, disciplined environment. Common Sense won a huge majority on an agenda centred around increased use of corporal punishment in schools and the justice system. I underestimated the opposition to doing what we had been given a mandate from the electorate to do. David McDougall's soft-heartedness came back to haunt me. It seemed to start a switch in public opinion, which grew and grew. It was such a pity because everyone would have benefitted from less crime, greater respect towards other people and a disciplined society."

Monique stands up at this point. "I can't sit any longer. I need a few minutes to walk around and hurt from somewhere other than my backside."

"Can I see the marks?"

"Why not. They are your handiwork." Monique unbuttons the blouse and steps out of the skirt, leaving her naked.

Bob walks slowly around her. "Not the best weapon

but it was all I could find. You look beautiful wearing stripes. Your breasts look bruised, and your buttocks are a bit swollen. You'll be much better tomorrow and in about a week the marks will have completely faded. The thing is, though, you are a different person today. Courteous, respectful and non-combative for a change. Everybody needs a firm hand now and again."

"Pity you chose a firm flex, isn't it? If we can finish your term in office today, that will leave us with the interview at Downing Street and prison. I would love to get all that done by tomorrow afternoon because Louise is arriving early evening."

"Excellent. I will get to meet her, at last. I hope I won't be disappointed."

"I hope so, too." Monique is walking around the room and has her back to Bob Godwin when she makes this remark. Because of this, he does not see the wry grin on her face. "I think I can bear those cushions again," she says, putting her clothes back on. "Work calls. I must ask you to explain the confusion about your policy on vegetarianism and veganism."

"That was unfortunate. At that time, several respectable organisations had printed papers suggesting that there were significant dangers in eating only a vegetarian or vegan diet. Many other countries, including France, incidentally, acted upon the reports but most stopped at giving advice on the risks. I simply made a mistake when writing the pronouncement and mentioned a ban instead of advice to reduce reliance on such foods. As soon as people started complaining, I realised what I had done and corrected the situation. Naturally, David McDougall tried to capitalise on the situation, saying that my mother had been scared by a cabbage. One newspaper had a picture on the front page of me with my head replaced by a cabbage. That highlighted another problem. I set up the Ministry of Decency to help prevent things like that being published. I wanted to ban pornography, nudity, obscenity and fake news from papers, radio and television. I had hoped in my second term to tackle the filth on the internet, in conjunction with other countries. It just didn't happen. I suppose I took my eye off that particular ball. Obviously, I appointed the wrong person to run it. Something else that would have been put right if I had been re-elected."

"I have two points arising from what you said. Many people were genuinely worried that the Ministry of Decency meant the start of total Government censorship. Could you comment on that, please? Secondly, you seemed to be interfering in other aspects of health as well as vegetarianism. You restricted the sale of cigarettes and confectionery and ordered everyone to eat red meat twice a week. Why was your Government so obsessed with people's shopping habits?"

"The health restrictions were put in place to improve the nation's health. Obesity and cancers caused by smoking are the two greatest enemies to the health of humans. There has been much advice over the years but no real progress. I decided it was time to become more proactive and introduce limits on certain items that are proven to damage health. The NHS, at the time, was still suffering from the Covid years. There is only so much money to spend on healthcare. If the number of patients can be reduced by eating better at home, then everybody benefits, and the NHS has beds available for the genuinely sick and emergencies."

"Or the flogged and branded from your punishment centres," interjects Monique.

"Beginning to get ever so slightly combative again, I see. Any improvement in a nation's overall health is a good thing. There will always be illness, that is inevitable, but even a slight reduction in smoking or eating more healthily automatically frees up beds. Regarding your point, an effective discipline system is bound to produce casualties. The way to avoid this is to ensure punishments are severe enough to deter people from misbehaving. The lower the crime rate, the fewer criminals to punish and a reduction in hospital beds needed to deal with flogging or branding injuries. Combined with improved health in the population, this reduces the pressures on the NHS and ultimately the economy. As regards your first point, the intention in forming the Ministry of Decency was to remove from circulation anything blasphemous, obscene or pornographic. You can call that censorship if you like but I call it common sense. No one is going to suffer if they can't access the pure filth that is around nowadays. I was shown magazines with pictures of two nude men kissing each other, a naked woman with a dog, and a young child watching a man and a woman having sex. It is pure filth. I failed to get rid of this rubbish, but it is a disgrace to a decent nation to have things like that available."

"I accept that, but people worried that your Ministry of Decency was the first step to them being allowed to see only certain approved things. The pornography you described is awful, but some people enjoy it, and they have the right to do so in any democratic society. You were trying to control people's eating habits, health, sex lives and what they can read or listen to. Can you understand the concerns over the direction you were taking?"

"Very delicately put. You're learning. There must be laws, there must be order. Otherwise, you have anarchy. I wanted to create a law-abiding, healthy, clean-living nation with no criminals, no pornography, no perverts and no dissention. There is nothing at all wrong with order."

"But you were dealing with human beings. We are used to making our own decisions and the vast majority do that quite satisfactorily for their whole lives. You cannot impose diet, sexual preference or good health on people. Every individual has their own way of doing things and that is what makes the world an interesting and exciting place. If you want world order and precision, I suggest you play model soldiers because the real world will never be ready for your kind of uniformity. I am me and you are you. Believe me, you would not want to be me, but I do. I like me and I certainly do not fit into your idea of a clean-living, vanilla automaton. I am bisexual. I enjoyed our fuck, but I would also quite willingly have shared my bed that night with a woman if one had offered. I have accepted money for sex but that is my choice. I have a mind of my own. I have had desperately bad times when I've been homeless and penniless through my own stupid decisions, but I have the right to do that. I've never been in trouble with the police. I have never deliberately hurt anyone and definitely not with an electric flex. I don't want to be forced into a mould and look and behave like everyone else so you can have the perfect utopian society. You can call me a pervert or a dissenter or whatever you like. You can beat me unconscious, but I will bounce back the same old me. That is why you failed. You understand discipline but you don't understand people. You broke my body last night, but you won't break my spirit or my determination to be me. As you found out, it only takes one or two people like David McDougall or Sara Molan to say, 'This is not right' and the small snowball gathers more and more support until it is a massive snowball threatening to knock down your house of straw. I genuinely believe you thought you were doing the right thing, but you hurt so many people in the process."

"That is your opinion. You would have benefitted from being in London when I was in power. My system would soon have beaten this bisexual nonsense out of you. I will not be shamed into feeling sorry for the criminals who were, for five years, properly punished. They were criminals. They got what they deserved. Human rights are overrated. Human wrongs cause misery to thousands every day, but nobody cares. Well, I care and when I am back in power you had better make sure you are living in a different country. Sexual perversion and prostitution – nobody of either sex would want you by the time you got out of prison. Repent your sins, Monique, before it is too late."

She ignores Bob's entreaty and cheerfully says, "We missed lunch and now it is time for dinner. Is there anything else you want to talk about relating to your years in power?"

"It is a pity my final interview with Sara Molan was never shown. I had some brilliant ideas for my second term, which would have benefitted the country hugely. With no leader and many of the Common Sense MPs defecting to David McDougall's new party, we still retained fifteen seats at the 2034 election. Just imagine how many we would have had if that interview had been on television and I had been able to canvass support as planned. I think we've covered that pretty well and, in fairness, you have given me plenty of time and opportunities to explain my decisions and my ideology."

"Tomorrow, then, we need to cover the interview you mentioned and your time in prison. Let's eat. I hope I have a better night than I did last night."

"Would you like some company tonight or are you still mad at me?"

"No and no," replies Monique as she heads into the kitchen.

*

The next morning, Monique is feeling quite a bit better, although the marks are still very visible and necessitate a repeat of yesterday's clothing. With the bedroom door firmly locked, she starts to pack up her possessions. Before putting anything into her suitcase, she retrieves an item, carefully secured in bubble wrap, and places it carefully in her handbag. Unbeknownst to Bob, she gathered up all the tapes the previous night and now puts them into a separate bag and places that on top of her suitcase. She then puts both securely away in her wardrobe.

The morning exercise today is walking the length of the beach at Monique's still reduced pace. Bob is full of questions about Louise Land.

"Do you think she'll like what we've done?"

"I hope so. I need the money. She will listen to the tapes and then probably ask you about anything you've said that she doesn't understand. Then I will work with her to type it all up as a book."

"Do you need me for that?"

"Had enough of me? The answer is yes, because we may need you to expand on some things or Louise may feel that some subjects could be reduced a little. It is your book, your autobiography, bearing your name, so we want you to be happy about what is included and what is excluded."

"When do I get paid?"

"That depends on what you agreed with Louise. I get paid when she is happy with the book. I suppose it's the same for you. Are you going back to England?"

"Don't think that would be a good idea. I'm not supposed to leave the country. I'll probably have to serve the remaining six years of my original sentence if I return. I'll find somewhere where I feel comfortable, and nobody cares about my past."

"How about Argentina? I hear they will take anybody and, of course, you did try to give them the Falklands Islands. You're probably a national hero over there."

The conversation peters out after that and they return in silence to start the last day of the first stage of writing Bob Godwin's autobiography.

"I would like you to tell me exactly what happened when Sara Molan went to Downing Street to interview you. Remember, no one has heard your side of the story because you pleaded guilty at trial. So, this is your first chance to put the record straight."

"The interview was arranged about a year in advance. I Insisted that it should be done my way. I wrote the questions and Sara agreed not to interrupt or make detrimental remarks."

"How did you get Sara Molan to agree to those conditions?"

"I threatened to reveal certain information about her private life, and I also had some leverage on her boss. They soon saw things my way."

"So, you blackmailed them?"

"Such a vulgar word. I persuaded them to do it my way. I have never seen the interview, but when we were recording I thought it was excellent and I feel that I was right to insist on trying something different. Sara arrived around seven thirty and we had a chat, and I had a drink, I believe. The interview went really well and then we had some food. I had some ham, but Sara didn't eat anything, though she had several glasses of champagne. I had never made any secret of my feelings for Sara and I asked her to marry me. She said no because she still loved Nic. I leant in to kiss her and she did not object, so I started to make love to her. I pulled her skirt down and then jokingly ripped her tights because I had asked her to wear stockings. I pulled her panties down and then suddenly she went berserk hitting me and screaming at me. She was hysterical and I slapped her across the face to calm her down. She tried to get out of the door, but it was locked. I don't know what happened after that. I remember someone shouting to be let in. Then the door burst open. Sara was on the ground bleeding and I was holding a bloodstained knife. I honestly don't know the sequence of events. I must have stabbed her because there was nobody else there. It torments me every day that I hurt someone I loved and still love. I could have made her happy."

"Did you know at that time that Sara Molan was gay?"

"No. I did not. I could have loved her so much better than that Nic woman."

"You were using her relationship with Nic to get her to do what you wanted but really you knew nothing about her private life at all. So, you tricked her into doing what you wanted and then, when she refused to marry you, tried to rape her."

"No. You've got it all wrong. The agreement was that I would keep quiet about her relationship, which I admit was even more disgusting than I suspected, and in return she would conduct the interview as I wanted it to be done and also sleep with me after the interview. I didn't try to rape her. She had consented by accepting the deal. She owes me a bonk, basically. I have no idea why she got so upset. If she had kept her end of the bargain, no damage would have been done."

"Do you really believe that a lesbian would volunteer to have sex with you?"

"It was one of her games. She was flirting with me during our first interview the day after the election victory. She wanted to please me by skewering McDougall when he was frothing at the mouth about that brain-damaged nobody Menzies sentenced to death. She would do anything when she wanted something, like an exclusive interview. Then, when she had got her way, all I got was silence and the cold shoulder. Then when I finally made my move, she had a total meltdown just when things were getting interesting. Good grief, what else could she have wanted? I even proposed marriage."

"Let me just understand this. You can't remember stabbing Sara or why you did it and all sexual contact that night was consensual. Is that your story?"

"Yes."

"What do you think Sara would say if she was here?"

"A pack of lies, no doubt."

"You said earlier that you still love her. But she represents everything you dislike. If you had caught her with another woman, you would have had her flogged repeatedly, branded and thrown into prison for years. You wanted to ban anything with any same-sex pictures. Don't you think that makes you a hypocrite?"

"I protected her. I knew she was having sex with Nic before the Justice Act was introduced. She failed to register that relationship. I knew she would fail a virginity test, so I removed her from the list. I saved her from the punishment you mentioned."

"So, a nasty little bit of old-fashioned corruption justifies blackmail and attempted rape."

"I wish you would listen, you stupid woman. I didn't try to rape Sara Molan. I didn't need to. She was gagging for it. No woman can last forever without a penis between their legs now and again. You proved that yourself. All this nonsense about being bisexual. You could have bedded the cleaner if you wanted a woman, but you know which side your bread is buttered. Go on, deny it."

"I think the cleaner is even older than you. Perhaps you would have been happier with her. Women have as much right as men to use their bodies in any way they like. I wanted and needed a man that night and you were available. You were okay, by the way, but you could improve your aftercare. Most men send flowers or perhaps a box of chocolates. You seem to offer a choice of a brutal whipping or being stabbed. Every woman is different. Just because I like men and women does not mean every woman does. Just because I had sex with you once does not mean I want you or any other man next time I feel like having sex. You need to start treating women as equals with feelings and needs. Equality is the name of the game now. Anybody can achieve anything they want if they are prepared to work for it, regardless of age, colour, circumstances and what sexual organs they were born with. That is the way it ought to be, and woe betide anyone, even you, who tries to take us back to the days when white males ruled the world."

"Behaving like this, I'm beginning to think you need another thrashing."

"Only if you want to lose your money. I think it is better for both of us if we agree to differ and move on. I would like you to talk about your time in prison."

"I really don't want to talk about that."

"I think you should. It is your big chance to win some sympathy from the readers and also show that you suffered terribly in paying for your mistakes."

"I'll try. That fool Menzies was determined to

punish me, even though I had his back over the Aaron Davis business. He insisted I should be remanded to prison. I ended up in Wandsworth. Just about everyone in the place seemed to have a grievance against me. They knocked my front teeth out so I couldn't bite anyone while I was giving head. I had things you would never believe stuck up my rear. I was punched, beaten and even taken from cell to cell naked and bleeding to be raped or abused. The prison officers miraculously disappeared every single time I was attacked. After two days of this appalling punishment, I knew I had to do something, so I asked the Governor to arrange for Chief Inspector Melville to come and see me. I told him I would be dead if something wasn't done to rescue me. So, we did a deal, and I am not ashamed to say that. I had not been sentenced to death and yet I was very close to dying at the hands of the animals I had been trying so hard to reform. I agreed to plead guilty to attempted murder in return for serving my sentence in solitary confinement. No flogging or branding and no attempted rape charge in return for a quick conviction. This time, even Menzies played along. Actually, thinking about it, Judge Menzies would be a brilliant subject for your next book. Someone who has never let a chance go past him to ruin some poor soul's life. Anyway, solitary confinement was a completely different type of nightmare. Twenty-three hours a day alone in my cell with just two half-hour exercise breaks. On my own, of course, apart from one bored prison officer. Same routine day after day, month after month and year after year. For six years."

"If Sir Keir Starmer hadn't won the 2034 election and repealed your Justice Act, you would have done twelve years and a lot more if you had been punished under your own rulebook."

"I think six years for something I do not remember doing is about right. Anyway, I am still suffering. Every time I close my eyes, I am back in Wandsworth prison being raped and abused."

"What about visitors?"

"Not one in six years. I was deserted by everyone. Nobody from my party has been in touch with me since I was arrested. I thought Sara would come but no such luck."

"You've mentioned occasionally that you regret some decisions, but do you think you owe the British people an apology for what happened during your five years in power?"

"I understand why you might think I should apologise, but I strongly disagree. Common Sense was voted into power to reduce crime and improve law and order. That was done. Criminals might be complaining about their sentences, but they are not pleading innocence. Ordinary people gained from restoring order and values. They do not need an apology and I flatly refuse to apologise to people who broke the law and paid the penalty."

"You admit to protecting people like Sara and her

boss from virginity tests and potential prosecution. Do you think that is acceptable?"

"In any country or society, some people will be more important than the vast majority of the population. I am talking about Government ministers, MPs belonging to the ruling party, top civil servants, judges, senior police officers, civil servants, military top brass and some media figures. Anybody, really, who is important to the smooth running of the nation day by day. This elite group must remain unhindered for the good of everyone. I needed Sara and Marshall in their jobs and compliant. Eventually, they would have become surplus to my requirements and then they would have had to face up to their crimes like the vast majority of the populace."

"Who else did you allow to break the law?"

"I am certainly not going to name names. I will say that a female Common Sense MP fell in love with a Conservative member, who was married. The party whips had a chat with her, and she finished the affair immediately. What was the point of taking the matter any further? She was removed from the list for virginity tests and that was that."

"Would you have done the same for, say, a waitress in the House of Commons restaurant?"

"Of course not. If I had been advised of a situation like that I would have got the Downing Street police under Inspector Plod to arrest her and her lover. She would have been charged with having sex whilst unmarried and the man would have faced an adultery charge."

"So, one rule for the elite and another rule for everybody else."

"Waitresses are ten a penny. They don't matter in the grand scheme of things. MPs are important and much harder to replace. Monique, don't look at me like that. It is how the world has always worked and always will."

"Despite turning a blind eye to the misdemeanours of your cronies, you really did do a great job in reducing crime rates. Eighty-three per cent reduction in your five year term, I believe. How did you manage that when you were introducing new crimes like adultery and sex outside marriage? How exactly were the reductions calculated?"

"This is a complicated subject. You are right in saying that there were more offences than ever before and certainly a significant increase in convictions and prisoners. Taking large numbers of offenders out of circulation is bound to reduce crime, since they can't break any more laws once they're in prison. It became so complicated trying to work out the figures that in the end I just thought up a realistic figure and used that in my pronouncements."

"Is there any limit to how low you are prepared to sink? I think that will do. Louise will be here in an hour or so. I'll cook something now, so it's all over and done with before she arrives."

"Do you think we should wait for her?"

"No. I'm hungry. If she wants something, I can easily get it whilst she talks to you."

"Is she staying here?"

"She'll be staying in whichever hotel is rated the best in the area. Actually, there is one thing we haven't done yet. Louise wants us to think of a title for the book. Any ideas?"

"'Common Sense'. 'The Real Bob Godwin'. 'The Bob Godwin Story'. 'The True Story Of Britain's Best Ever Prime Minister'. 'Justice And Me'. What do you think?"

"I think that is the most interested and vocal you have been all week. I quite like 'The Real Bob Godwin' or 'The Bob Godwin Story'. The rest we can forget, I think. No one in their right mind would call a book 'Common Sense'. Just forget you ever mentioned the other two. How about, 'From Cars To Bars' or 'How To Annoy An Entire Country Without Even Trying'?"

"I will decide as you are clearly trying to annoy me, again. We will go with 'The Real Bob Godwin'."

"Fine. I'll be in the kitchen if you need me."

CHAPTER 3

LOUISE

18 June 2040

Bob becomes increasingly quiet and nervous as he awaits Louise's arrival. Monique is quite openly excited about being reunited with an old friend. At seven thirty, the doorbell rings. Monique goes to answer it and Bob hears whispered conversation between the two women, without being able to catch more than the occasional word.

Monique enters the living room first and Louise Land follows. Bob Godwin stares in disbelief at the newcomer. "What the hell are you doing here, Sara? Where's my publisher?"

"You've changed since I last saw you. You look much older and careworn. I gather you had a hard time in prison. The only pity is you only served six years. From my point of view, you got away with it. Stabbing me twice and trying to rape me and six years later here we are. You totally free and me, the innocent victim, still serving my sentence of nightmares and fear every time I go anywhere." Godwin starts to rise but Sara Molan produces a pistol and points it at his head. "Sit down or I will shoot."

"You haven't got the guts."

"Sit down and don't move or you will find out, won't you?"

Bob sits down.

"What's going on here? Where's Louise Land?"

"You're looking at her. I knew you would do anything for a big fee and a chance to put your side of the story across. I don't think you would have been so keen if I had sent you a letter asking you to meet me in Paris. Mind you, it was a bit naughty leaving Britain when you were on parole. I think I should formally introduce my beautiful accomplice here, Monique. Bob Godwin, please meet Nicolette Du Bois, or Nic as she is generally known."

"Alright, so you tricked me, and now I'm in the company of two lesbian sluts. So? What in God's name is the point of all this?"

"We thought we'd see whether you had matured and perhaps realised the damage you caused to so many people. We don't have the strength or the cocks to deal with you like the Wandsworth prisoners did, but we will do our best. Nic, how has he come across in the days you've been here alone with him?"

"Absolutely no regret for anything, except that some restrictions like the Ministry of Decency and the attack on vegetarians did not produce the right results. I showed him a couple of the photos you sent, but he didn't give a damn about them or the people pictured. Personally, he has been charming when he wanted sex and a dangerous sadist when he decided to whip me."

Sara interrupts. "Nic, come round this side and show me your back. Then I can see the damage without taking my eyes off my target."

Nic comes round as requested and pulls her blouse up to reveal the still very bright red welts and cuts crisscrossing her back.

Sara addresses Bob, "That's two or three days after you attacked her. You should be truly ashamed of yourself."

"Well, I'm not. She deserved it. She was combative, rude and showed me no respect. I will tell you what I have already told Nic, back when she was Monique. Humans need to be trained to behave. Discipline is how you achieve that. I would not say she has been perfect since, but overall her behaviour did improve. She will remember the lesson for the rest of her life."

"Nic, do you want your revenge and whip him whilst I am standing here pointing a gun at him?"

"Non. He's not worth it. He has been arrogant, sexist and will not accept that he mistreated an entire nation. He wants to call the book 'The True Story Of Britain's Best Ever Prime Minister' and also he did admit to protecting you, your boss and anyone else he considered important or useful."

"How did you protect me then Bob? You didn't protect me from the maniac who nearly killed me."

"I knew you were living with Nic. You were on a list of people who had not reported a prior relationship. You were going to be called in for a virginity test. When you had failed it, you would have been jailed, flogged and probably branded. I couldn't let that happen to the girl I loved and still love. So, I took you off the list and you were left in peace. You should be really thankful."

Nic continues with her summary of Bob's comments during their time together. "He said several times that he still loves you and also that you consented to sex with him. In fact, he said you were gagging for it."

"Right, well, Bob, you have been telling your side of the story. I now want you to sit quietly and listen to our stories. You can comment at the end and remember I still have a gun pointing at you," says Sara. "Nic, do you want to go first?"

"Sure. I used to be a model, firstly in Paris and then in London. Bob, you would dismiss most of my photographs as pornographic, but I have never been ashamed of my body. I was very successful in London and made a lot of money. I met Sara in a club in 2026. It was love at first sight for both of us. She was not earning much at the time but was working so hard to climb the ladder and become a TV presenter. I was so proud when she hosted her first show and when she replaced

David McDougall. Sara proposed to me in 2028 and I accepted. We were so happy. We were both doing well in our careers and so wonderfully happy. I was working in Scotland when you came to power. Within days, you casually destroyed our lives. Just because I fell in love with another woman, I was suddenly a criminal facing prison and torture. Sara and I broke up immediately. I went back to Paris and tried to get modelling work. My face just didn't fit anymore. I became a street prostitute briefly, then I met a man who asked me to become his mistress. He paid my rent, gave me gifts or money and expected me to sleep with him whenever he wanted. That man died but there were others. After about three years, I moved to Lyon. I had a relationship with a woman there, but it ended and I moved to Marseilles. I pretended I was happy, but really my life was meaningless without Sara. She rang me a few times in the months leading up to you attacking her. She was terrified of you and desperate to avoid having sex with you. I have already told you I am bi, but Sara has never been with a man and she definitely did not want to start with you. She rang me before she went into Downing Street that night and asked me to ring the police and get them to rescue her. The officers were just too late to stop her being stabbed but just in time to save her life. When I was told, I flew straight to London. I spent days sitting by Sara's bedside, holding her hand and talking to her. I prayed for her to survive. As soon as she was fully conscious, I proposed and she said, 'Yes'. Sara went through six months of physiotherapy, rehabilitation and counselling. When that was over, we went back to Paris. I found work as front of house in restaurants, but Sara found it difficult to do very much. Doctors said she was fine, but she wasn't. There was always something stopping her being happy. We talked and talked but we always came back to the same thing. Bob Godwin. Sara needs closure by meeting you face to face and the two of us telling you what you did to us and untold others. As Sara said earlier, the only way we could arrange that was to trick you and I apologise for the deception. It will be worth it if she can finally move on and be happy again. You are a cruel man. I know now that you had a dreadful childhood and that you were let down by every woman you loved. Taking it out on an entire nation and especially the gay community, prostitutes and adulterers was never going to erase your painful memories. You just managed to ruin thousands and thousands more lives. They can't all be here to confront you, but I have shown you photographs of some of your victims and now you are listening to two more. I want you to understand and apologise to both of us. Then, maybe, we can start our lives again, together."

As she finishes, Nic looks over to Sara, who is wiping away tears with one hand, whilst still aiming the gun at Godwin with the other. Ms Molan composes herself and starts speaking. "Thank you, Nic. You brought me to tears. We will find out later if it affected our guest. I was brought up in India. When I became a teenager, I knew

I did not feel attracted to men. By the age of fourteen I knew I fancied women. I was too scared to tell anybody. At eighteen I was at college and one of the students there became friendly with me. One day she kissed me, and everything seemed so right. We started to have sex. I had no idea then what to do but she was very patient and showed me various techniques and positions. I loved her so much. A few weeks after we met, we were having sex in my bedroom when my mother walked in and caught us. I thought she was going to have a heart attack. She threw my girlfriend out of the house and chucked her clothes after her. She screamed at me and by nightfall I was homeless and had lost my family for ever. I knew I would be in danger once more people locally heard what I had done. I worked while at college, so I had some money. I decided to leave India but had no idea where to go. My family had always told me I had English ancestors, so I caught a flight to London. Luck was on my side. Britain then helped refugees who faced persecution in their own country. I was allowed to stay and given a flat to live in. I finished college in London and then went to university. Part-time work helped me pay my own way. After university, I started in television at the very bottom and worked my way up. I was still nearer the bottom of the ladder than the top when I met Nic. There had been a few short romances, but she was my first serious affair since India. We moved in together and everything was perfect. My career took off, I started earning really good money and we got engaged. Then Common Sense won the 2029 election and my personal life just fell apart. Nic and I split up. I concentrated on my work but then you started messing with my mind. Sending me flowers, professing your love and promising me an exclusive interview if I just made David McDougall look a fool. Then, after that exclusive interview rebounded on you, the threats started. You would expose my affair with Nic. I have always jealously guarded my private life. You fooled me. I genuinely thought you knew the truth. It was a year between you blackmailing me and the actual interview at Downing Street. You tortured me mentally throughout that time with menacing texts and constant reminders that I was expected to sleep with you as part of the deal. Nic is right, I was terrified of you and of what you might do to me. I tried to get William Marshall to help me escape from your clutches, but you scared him off. So, I turned to Nic for help. It almost worked but you threw me off balance by proposing. I said no because I still loved her. That annoyed you and you started badmouthing Nic. That was your big mistake because you referred to her as "He" and "Himself". I just got so angry. A whole year of being blackmailed and taunted by you and you knew nothing. You had nothing on me because you didn't even know Nic's gender. I could have quite easily killed you there and then. The problem was that by forcing your hand then, everything happened more quickly than I had expected. I remember attacking you, but you hit me and pushed me against the wall. You started undressing me. You got my skirt down. Then you got annoyed because I was wearing tights and you ripped them to pieces. Then you pulled my panties down and held me against the wall and then you started to rape me. Let me make it clear. I have never had sex with a man, and I had absolutely no intention of starting that night. I consented to nothing. You tried to penetrate me. You tried to rape me. I managed to push you away and ran to the door. It was locked, so I started screaming for help. You dragged me away from the door. You had a big knife in your hand. I remember a dreadful pain. The next thing I remember is waking up days later in hospital with Nic holding my hand. I agree with everything Nic has said about the last six years. I have suffered and I have made her suffer with me. I just want to be happy and start to live again. Only you can help me do that by admitting you blackmailed me, you tortured me mentally and that you knew full well that I did not want to have sex with you."

"I obviously feel sympathy with you both if you have really suffered for the last six years, but I suffered grievously as well. I do not regret the general direction I took when in power. Some policies could have been better, and I made mistakes along the way. You came on to me, Sara. Your own behaviour has led to your distress. You would still, probably, be in India with your family if you were not a pervert. Whether you admit it or not, you came on to me. You led me on and then got cold feet. Welcome to the real world, which doesn't revolve entirely around Sara Molan. I am not going to apologise to you. Why should I? If anything, you should be apologising to me for this ridiculous trick you played on me. Just leave me alone and sod off and lead your miserable lives blaming everyone else but yourselves."

Sara replies extremely calmly. "I cannot live my life properly until there is closure one way or another. It is up to you. I am going to give you the gun."

"*Sara, don't be stupid.*" Nic cries out, agitatedly.

"You have two choices then. Do the decent thing and shoot yourself or end my torment by shooting me."

Sara pushes the gun across the desk to Bob. He picks it up and aims at his accuser. "Goodbye, Sara," he says and pulls the trigger.

Nothing happens.

Whilst this has been going on, Nic, unseen, takes her gun out of her handbag and moves close to Godwin.

Sara laughs evilly. "Did you really think I would give you a loaded gun? Nic has the one with bullets in it."

Before Bob Godwin can react, Nic pulls the trigger once and he falls forward onto the desk with blood pouring from the left side of his head. She checks the body and confirms to Sara, "He's dead. It's over at last. You were brilliant."

They embrace and then Nic wipes her fingerprints off the gun with a handkerchief. Then using the handkerchief to prevent any more prints, she pushes the gun and then the trigger into Godwin's lifeless hands. After mentally measuring a couple of distances, she carefully places the gun on the floor in the position she calculates it would have landed if a suicide had taken place. Sara is busy packing up the recorder and the remaining tapes.

Nic dashes upstairs and collects her suitcase and the bag containing the earlier tapes. "How are we doing for time?" she asks Sara.

"Fine for the ferry but I think we should get out of here. Someone may have heard that shot and called the police. I don't think I want to explain this to a gendarme."

Nic has a quick check around to make sure that they haven't left anything incriminating behind and then they both head out to make a fresh start in their lives. Together.

CHAPTER 4

CLAUDE

Last Week of June 2040

"Chief Inspector, there is a French police officer on the phone asking to speak to you."

"Thank you. Put him through, please," says CI Melville, slightly puzzled. "Bonjour. How can I help you?"

"Bonjour. I hope you can. You are the sixth person I've spoken to. My name is Lieutenant Claude Abbeye from the Calais police. Last week we were called to a suicide in a rented villa on the beachfront. The deceased had a passport in the name of Robert Harris. The picture in the passport matches the victim. An officer thought he recognised the man, and we are fairly confident that he is actually Robert Godwin, your ex-Prime Minister. Are you interested?"

"Very. I led the investigation that put Godwin in jail.

He came out about two months ago. He was not allowed to travel abroad without permission. If you can send me a picture of the deceased and the passport photo, I will give you a positive identification or not, as the case may be."

"That explains the passport. Do you have any idea why he would be in Calais?"

"None at all. Is this definitely a suicide?"

"On first look, definitely. Everything is exactly right. One shot to the head. Body slumped on desk. Gun in exactly the right position. As we go deeper, some other things emerge. The body was found by the cleaner when she started work in the morning. She says that there was a man and a woman living there for about a week. She never saw them. She does not know for certain if the body was the man staying there or not. No sign of a woman having been there recently. We found an electric cable in the living room. It has traces of human blood and flesh on it. Not the victim's. The villa was rented by a Louise Land. She told the owner she was a publisher in Paris. Everything was arranged by e-mail, telephone or post. The address given does exist, but nobody there has heard of this woman or her publishing company. The e-mail account was closed on the day the man died. It looks like suicide and in seven days it will be ruled to be suicide, but something smells wrong here."

"I think so too. Godwin was very badly attacked and sexually abused on remand. He arranged a deal to get away from his attackers and spent six years in solitary confinement at his own request. He never once attempted to kill himself in prison. Why on earth would he commit suicide just after his release? It makes no sense at all. What time was he killed?"

"Somewhere between eight PM and midnight on the eighteenth of June."

"Do you have late-night ferries between Calais and Britain at this time of year?"

"I will check for you."

"If there are any such ferries, can you send me the passenger list? I will see if any names ring a bell."

"Oui, monsieur."

"Can you also look into a couple of other things please? Did anyone see Godwin with someone in the days before he was killed? On the beach, perhaps, or in the shops?"

"We've tried that. He was seen several times with a younger woman. I could do a great picture of her legs and her breasts, but her face – not a chance. She sunbathed nude or topless and not one passer-by took any interest in her face, just her body. Same in the shops. Paid for everything by cash."

"That is interesting. Keeping away from the cleaner and trying to avert attention away from her face. That seems suspicious to me. If this is ruled as suicide, can we still investigate?"

"Mais oui. We can reopen the case at any time. Do you have an idea?"

"Maybe, maybe not. The girlfriend of Sara Molan,

the woman Godwin stabbed, vowed revenge. When I met her six years ago, she could stop traffic without even trying. An incredibly beautiful woman with a wonderful figure. I will try to find out if they are back in London. I would be very suspicious if their names appear on a ferry passenger list for that day. I'll send you an e-mail with what information I would like and my contact details. I will confirm with my boss that she is happy for me to get involved in this. But that should be a formality."

"I will e-mail you the pictures. Could you let me know if it is or if it is not Robert Godwin?"

"Yes, of course. Au revoir."

"Au revoir."

A few minutes later, Melville receives an e-mail from Claude containing the passport picture and a photograph of the deceased taken at the villa. After looking at the pictures, he picks up the phone and dials. "Can I speak to Commissioner Giles, please? I'm CI Melville."

"Giles speaking. What can I do for you?"

He explains the previous phone call and then says, "The deceased is definitely Robert 'Bob' Godwin. His is also the photograph in the passport of Robert Harris."

"To be frank, I do not think many people will be shedding tears for him. What do you think?"

"It looks exactly like a suicide, Ma'am, and that's the problem. It looks too precise, too measured and there are so many loose ends. Why was Godwin in Calais in breach of his parole conditions? It must have been important to risk another six years in solitary. Who was the mystery woman shopping and sunbathing with him? Why was there blood and flesh on an electric cable?"

"Do you want to run with this for a bit? The last thing I want to do is ignore the possible murder of a former Prime Minister, even if it is Godwin."

"Thank you, Ma'am. I'll keep you informed of progress."

*

A week later, another call comes through from Lieutenant Abbeye. He starts the conversation. "I have just sent over the passenger list from the midnight ferry from Calais to Dover on the date of the death."

"Yes, I've just opened the e-mail. I'm just quickly looking down the list. Well, that is interesting. Ms Sara Molan and Ms Nicolette Du Bois were on that ferry."

"Coincidence?"

"I don't believe in them. This is your case, Claude. What do you want me to do?"

"Could you go and see them, if indeed they are in London? I do not think we should be too heavy. You know them, so you would be the ideal person to make gentle enquiries. We have a very solid case for suicide, so the truth is we are trying to tie up loose ends. Nothing more than that."

"I don't really do gentle, but I will see what I can

do. Godwin's death has been announced over here, so I imagine they are expecting a visit sooner or later. All I've got to do is find out where they are, if they are in this country at all. I'll come back to you when I know something."

*

Two days later, after a brief telephone conversation with Nic, Melville finds himself drinking tea with Sara and her fiancée, in their newly rented Kensington apartment.

"This is a lovely property. How long have you been here?" he asks, innocently.

"About two weeks. We arranged to rent it unseen, and it was ready for us to move into as soon as we came back from Paris," replies Sara.

"What made you decide to come back?"

This time, it is Nic who answers. "It has taken a long time for Sara to fully recover. The wounds healed quickly but mentally it took much, much longer. I've been working in restaurants as front of house to earn money, but poor Sara has hardly been outside in nearly six years. A few months ago, she finally started to improve. We were so happy here in London before that, we decided to start again. So here we are."

"Are you aware that Robert Godwin is dead?"

"Yes," says Sara. "It's been in the papers and on the TV news. Suicide, apparently. I'm sorry, Chief Inspector, but I find it hard to feel sorry for him. He robbed me of six years of my life. Our lives, to be honest. There are so many people still suffering every day because of his sadism and cruelty."

"My boss said there would be few tears shed for him. Did either of you have any contact with him after he was arrested?"

"Of course not. I have been traumatised by what happened. Six months ago, I would have had a panic attack just talking to you about him. The last thing I wanted was to see him again."

Nic intervenes. "It's all right, Sara, he cannot hurt you now. What is this about, Chief Inspector?"

"Totally routine, nothing to worry about. The French police asked me to speak to you. His death has been ruled as suicide but there are one or two loose ends. Godwin died between eight PM and midnight on the eighteenth of June in a rented villa in Calais. He had been seen in recent days with a beautiful dark-haired woman, much younger than him. The villa had been rented by a publisher called Louise Land. She has vanished without trace, as indeed has whoever was spotted with Godwin. At midnight that night, the two of you caught a ferry from Calais to Dover. I don't like coincidences and it does seem interesting that you were in Calais the night he died. We were wondering if you had gone to see him. Perhaps you managed to get through to him how much misery he had caused, and he then committed suicide after you left?"

Sara replies, calmly. "I'm sorry, but this is pure

coincidence. We did leave Calais that night, but we had no idea Godwin was there too. We booked the tickets about a month ago, when we found out the date this flat would be available. We had to leave France from somewhere. There are no ferries from Paris to London, you know. We decided it might be safer to do the longer journey in France. We haven't driven in England for six years, so we thought we'd get reacquainted with driving on the left on a short journey with little traffic. It is just a coincidence, I'm afraid. As I said earlier, I have had no contact with Godwin since he stabbed me, and I have been more than happy to keep it that way."

"What about you, Nic? The description of the mysterious woman could possibly resemble you."

"I was with Nic in Paris. I quit work two weeks before we left and spent the time packing up six years of our lives. Six unhappy years because of that man. I never wanted to see him again."

"When you were in London in 2034, you swore revenge on Godwin."

"Did I? Well, we all say things in the heat of the moment. I hated him for what he did to Sara, but in a strange way he brought us back together. We are devoted to each other now and just want to move forward."

"Whilst Godwin was in jail, you chose to remain in France. Around the time he was released, you decide to come back here. Logically, it should have been the other way round. Sara, if you were so traumatised, why would you come back to the city where Godwin lived?"

"I see your point, Chief Inspector. Listen, I consider you a friend. You and your team saved my life. I cannot carry on calling you Chief Inspector. What is your first name?"

"Paul."

"Right then, Paul. I suffered nightmares and trauma for well over five years. Nic became my carer. Eventually all the counselling and treatments like CBT worked. I could see things differently and in a few weeks I gained confidence and started to live again. Nic is beautiful and deserves to be a top model. She has never fitted in with the French idea of what a model should look like. She stands a much better chance of finding work here. I have never worked on TV anywhere but Britain. So, if we are going to start again, it may as well be where we are known and have much better career opportunities. It was a risk while Godwin was alive, but I believed I could cope. Obviously, it is better now he is dead, but we had nothing to do with it. We arrived in Calais just after ten and drove straight to the ferry port. We did not go anywhere, and we saw nothing of Calais except moonlight, the main road and the port. Are we suspects?"

"No. There is no crime here if he took his own life. The Lieutenant dealing with this in Calais doesn't like coincidences either, so he asked me to see if you had visited Godwin whilst you were in Calais. Would either of you have any idea why an electric cable flex in the villa contained small traces of human flesh and blood?"

Sara laughs and says, "Nic, your field, I think."

"Some men like to introduce violence into their sex lives. With most, it goes no further than mild spanking. After the way Godwin embraced dreadfully severe floggings and beatings when he was Prime Minister, I think it is quite feasible that he carried that over into his private life. I imagine he whipped somebody, female presumably, with the flex. I can assure you that neither Sara nor I have been whipped recently. It is not something we need to do to get us excited. Would you like us to strip so you can check? Look, Sara, he's blushing. I managed to embarrass him several times six years ago. Some things do not change."

Melville laughs nervously. "No, please keep your clothes on. As I said before, Godwin's death is officially accepted as a suicide. That may change if further evidence is found later. You, clearly, are not involved so I am sorry to have troubled you and I hope you can now move forward. What are your plans?"

Sara replies, "I am going back to my old job. I spoke to William Marshall a couple of days ago. He is unhappy with his current presenter, so I start in August."

"You feel you can work with him? He did let you down six years ago."

"Marshall is alright. He got tangled up with Godwin just like I did. Anyway, these days it is all about ticking boxes. I am exactly what he needs to keep the PC department off his back. Ethnic minority, tick. Gay, tick. Older but not too old, tick. Female, tick. Know all of my boss's secrets, tick. It is very easy to get back in if you fit the right profile. I am not being rude, Paul, but as an older white, straight male, you have no chance on television. What an idiot. I am making judgements now. Are you straight?"

"Yes, I am. Happily married for over thirty years."

"How many years do you think we'll last, Nic?"

Despite the question not being directed at him, it is Melville who replies, "Are you thinking of tying the knot, then?"

"It is high on our list. We're looking at some venues where we can marry and hold the reception at the same place," replies Sara. "You must come with your wife and Sergeant Adams must come too. There would not be a wedding if he had not acted so quickly that night. We'll send you both an invitation when we have a date. Have you ever been to a same-sex wedding, Paul?"

"No, that will definitely be a new experience. Nic, what are your plans?"

"When we've settled back in properly, I'll ring some of my old contacts in the modelling world. I think I'm too old for nude and glamour work these days, but I would love to do advertising shoots, perhaps even for television. Of course, we've got the wedding to arrange, as well. We've been engaged for six years, so it is about time. It will be amazing to marry in London. Can I ask something about Godwin?"

"Of course."

"Do you know what he was doing in Calais?"

"The French police have got no idea whatsoever.

That is why they would like to talk to the woman who was apparently with him. He was not supposed to leave the country. So, it must have been something very important for him to risk going back to prison. I can't really imagine he would have taken that chance just to meet up with a prostitute. I fear it will forever be a mystery. I must be going. Thank you for the tea and I wish you well, Sara, with your television work. And you, Nic, with the modelling."

Sara replies, with a broad smile, "Look out for the wedding invitation."

When CI Melville has left the apartment, Sara and Nic hug each other. "I think that went very well," says Sara. "The death is accepted as suicide and they have no idea why Godwin was there. I doubt if we will hear any more about it."

"It was a masterstroke to invite him to the wedding. We can update ourselves on what is happening," replies Nic.

"What would you have done if he had asked you to strip? You've still got scars from the whipping that bastard Godwin gave you."

"I knew he would say no. Chief Inspector Melville backs away from anything remotely to do with sex or nudity. I would have had to make up some kind of story about a violent customer whilst I was on the match in Paris."

"Game, darling. On the game."

"These English expressions. I'll never understand this language. Why can't they all speak French like the rest of Europe?"

"Come on, Nic, we've got wedding arrangements to make."

*

Back in his office, Melville speaks to Claude Abbeye.

"I've been to see them. Butter wouldn't melt with those two. Had no idea Godwin was in Calais. Didn't have any contact with him after he was arrested. Booked the ferry weeks ago. They left from Calais because they would rather make a long journey in France than England. They did suggest that the flex had been used as a whip. Nic even suggested they should strip off to show me they hadn't been flogged recently."

"Did you take them up on the offer?"

"No, I did not. I've got my pension to think about. I'm not about to be in a flat with two naked women."

"Did you believe them?"

"Not a single word. They even used the word coincidence to explain their presence in Calais when Godwin died. I'm sure they know more than they are letting on. Believe it or not, they have invited me to their wedding. I bet you they ask me how your investigation is going."

"You couldn't get me an invitation, could you? I've never been to a same-sex wedding."

"Neither have I. I'll tell you all about it, if and when it happens."

CHAPTER 5

GEORGE

August and September 2040

Sara Molan is nervous. She keeps telling herself that everyone will understand if she is rusty after six years away, but she does not want understanding. She wants to reclaim her crown as the queen of daytime politics. There has been massive publicity about her return and now the pressure is on to deliver both a superb programme and massive ratings. Her dressing room resembles Kew Gardens, including a beautiful bouquet of white roses from Nic.

She walks out into the studio, considers slipping out through a fire exit and heads for her hot seat.

William Marshall approaches her. "Great to have you back, Sara. As you know, we have David McDougall on first. The Shadow Health Secretary has called off with hay fever, apparently. So, we've got the Speaker of the House Of Commons, George Montague, in to talk about his concerns that the monarchy is interfering with the role of Parliament. He is pricklier nowadays than he's ever been. If you think he's going too far, just cut to a break and lay the law down to him before you're on air again. Is it true you and Nic are getting married?"

"Yes, we are. Next month at a wedding venue in Greenwich. We really must get the invitations out. Typical of me, I've had six years off and done nothing. Now I'm back at work and trying to arrange a wedding at the same time. You should get an invitation by the end of the week. It's up to you who you bring as your plus one, just as long as it's not that little redhead Godwin told me about."

She smiles sweetly as an unhappy-looking William Marshall retreats to the safety of the control room.

Sara is soon joined by David McDougall. They do not get off to a good start conversationally as both start to say "Sorry" at exactly the same moment. Sara laughs and says, "You first. I'm supposed to be the host here."

"I was just going to say sorry to you. I feel I let you down the night you were stabbed. If only I had been able to take the call, I would have gone right round there and knocked that so-and-so out cold. I'm sorry for everything you've been through since that night."

"David, it's fine. I rang Nic when you didn't answer. She rang the police, but things moved quicker than I expected, and they arrived just after Godwin stabbed me. It's all in the past now. Nic and I are together forever now. Anyway, I am the one who owes you the apology. I let you down horribly when I interviewed you about Aaron Davis. Godwin promised me an exclusive interview if I messed up your campaign against the death penalty. I was a fool, and I betrayed the one person who helped me in my career. I'm so sorry. If I could go back eight years, I would in a heartbeat."

"It's absolutely fine. I forgave you years ago. You redeemed yourself anyway by ripping Godwin to shreds in that exclusive chat. I begged Marshall to let me be the first guest on your return. I've missed you and I've missed being challenged at interviews."

"It's my first day back and it's you, so I shall be super nice."

"No, you don't. We all need the old Molan inquisition back."

"Alright but don't you dare walk out on me again. Deal?"

"Deal."

"If we are friends again, can I ask you a massive favour? Would you give me away at my wedding next month? I have no family and very few friends outside of work and most of them seem to have moved on whilst I've been away. I will understand if you say no but you're the nearest thing to a father I've had since I was eighteen. Please."

"I ought to make you beg, but I really would love to give you away. I suppose Nic hasn't got any friends or family here either?"

"She has decided to have two bridesmaids and she is arranging for two of her old friends from her previous modelling career in London to do that."

"Where are you going for your honeymoon?"

"We're not. I don't think William Marshall will think much of me wanting weeks off next month to travel the world after six years on holiday. I am hoping to grab a few days off, so we can be together at home but no once-in-a-lifetime adventure."

The floor manager shouts, "One minute to air. Silence now please."

Soon, the theme music begins and then Sara speaks to the audience. "Hello and welcome to the weekday politics programme. My name is Sara Molan, and I am delighted to be back after six years away. I am even more delighted to welcome, as my first guest, a gentleman who is also returning after a break of several years. A former host of this very programme, Mr David McDougall, leader of the Liberty Party. David, it is lovely to see you and belated congratulations on your party's success in last year's elections. You now hold seventy-three seats having effectively merged with the remaining MPs from the now defunct Common Sense Party. Do you feel you can bridge the gap between the two main parties and yourselves and seriously challenge for power?"

"Hello, Sara. It is lovely to see you back where you belong. I am, of course, delighted with the progress Liberty has made since being formed six years ago. I think it has taken a while for the electorate to accept that our policies are entirely different to those of the Common Sense Party. Whilst I still believe that the only way to tackle crime is through tougher sentences, Liberty has no intention whatsoever of bringing back the death penalty or using corporal punishment in schools or the legal system. However, I do feel it is fair that sentences handed down by judges should be served in full and that prisons need to be places for reforming prisoners and offering educational opportunities as well as providing punishment. We also stand for urgent action to make this country carbon neutral and are totally supportive of green policies."

"Does any of that really distinguish you from the Labour Government and the Conservative opposition?"

"I think so. Only the Green Party matches our desire to save the planet and make Britain a leading nation in environmental matters. I believe that the British electorate have realised that they can trust me. I spent five years opposing the Common Sense Government, virtually without support. Time has shown that I was right to leave the party I co-founded and go it alone, so to speak. I am constantly striving to do better, and I believe that Liberty can make further inroads into the present two-party system."

"Strictly speaking, you were thrown out of Common Sense rather than leaving of your own volition."

"I am sorry. I forgot I am dealing with the queen of pedantry. You are quite right. I was thrown out of Common Sense, but the reason I was dismissed was that I was openly criticising the extremely severe nature of the Government's law and order policies."

"I don't think I have ever been described as the queen of anything before, so thank you. Perhaps we can now talk about your views of Sir Keir Starmer's Labour Government."

"Do we have to? Six years ago, Labour made a brilliant start by repealing the Justice Act 2029 in full. Since then, however, it has been downhill all the way. Britain is lagging behind other industrial powers in the use of new technology, industrial growth is stagnant, and we are in the middle of a costly and painful recession. Employment is falling, benefit payments are rising dramatically and, most worrying, of all is the cosying up of the Government to the EU. Leaving them in the first place almost tore this proud country apart. The remainers have not gone away, even after so many years. They are holding ministerial posts in our present Government. One result of this has been the almost total dismantling of our special relationship with the USA at a time when they are thriving economically."

"As you and many of today's audience know, I have been living in France for some years and have seen this increasing closeness from the other side, so to speak. The EU has struggled without the UK. They do not particularly like us, but they need us financially and especially as a trade partner, historically importing more than we sell in Europe. The view in France is that we will hold another referendum within two years and, all being well, will reapply for full membership within five years from the present date."

"That is my greatest nightmare and I wish to appeal now to the British public to wake up and smell the tea before it is too late, and we are once again pouring billions of pounds of this country's money into an organisation where we have few friends and even less influence."

"My next guest today is the Speaker of the House of Commons. He has been very vocal in recent months about the drop in standards in Parliament and also what he sees as the growing interference by the monarchy in political matters. Where do you stand on this issue?"

"Parliament is full of complicated procedures and centuries-old traditions. Some of them actually prevent or delay MPs from carrying out their core functions, to debate Government legislation and agree the way forward on the major issues facing the country. Disputes between Westminster and the Crown are centuries old. Remember Oliver Cromwell. Hopefully, any current problems can be resolved much more amicably. I know George Montague's views on these matters, and I think you could have quite a lively debate with him."

"You mentioned green and environmental issues earlier, but what policies do you have on these matters? Your manifesto for last year's election was devoid of any detail on this matter, so perhaps you could enlighten us all to your plans?"

"It is no good us taking unitary action on this

subject. The entire world needs to work together to resolve the issues here. I will outline some of the areas where improvement is needed urgently and our ideas to achieve this. It is sixteen years since this country was supposed to ban petrol and diesel cars in favour of electric vehicles. It is time that this initiative was revived. That would achieve a major reduction in pollution and represent a huge step towards a greener, cleaner Britain."

"That changeover to electric vehicles collapsed because the public did not want to participate. The three negative factors were the maximum mileage between charges, a lack of charging stations and the prohibitive cost of the electric cars. Very little has changed since then. If you want everyone to drive greener cars, then don't you have to tackle those three areas first?"

"What we need to do is commit to this project. The Government needs to spend money on improving the support network and offering price concessions to electric car producers. It always comes down to money, but the greatest threat to our civilisation is climate change. I call upon this government to tackle all these issues urgently and with proper funding."

"That is fine talk. The reality is that Labour have an overall majority and can do what they like. They are not interested in saving our planet. They would rather cosy up to the Unions. You simply do not have enough MPs to force the Government to pay any attention at all to what you say."

"The reality is that the opposition parties must work

together and ensure that the Government hears what changes the public wants. It is not impossible to steer Labour in a different direction, but it does take a long time and a lot of hard work."

"Finally, David, what is your position on HS2?"

"I am against it and always have been. I would oppose any attempt to resurrect the project. The Conservatives are against it on cost grounds. Labour scrapped the idea back in 2034, mainly because there were plans afoot to change the name of the project as a tribute to Bob Godwin. I do hear rumours around Westminster that Labour are keen to have another look at it. I hope that is not the case."

"Thank you very much, David."

"Sara, if I can just interrupt a second. I am sure that most of today's viewers are very aware of what you have been through in the last six years. It is marvellous to see you back where you belong and in fine form, being pedantic, irritating and knowledgeable at the same time. I hope you will forgive me for saying this. If anyone deserves happiness, then it is you. I am delighted you are marrying your long-term partner, Nic, in the near future. I wish you a long and successful marriage and I am sure the viewers want to be included in those wishes."

Sara seems emotional and close to tears, "Forgive me. I just need a minute to recover. Um, David, that was very kind of you. I didn't know you were going to say that, but it means a tremendous amount to Nic and myself. As I was saying, thank you very much for being my first guest. Mr David McDougall, informative and entertaining as always. I will be back in a few minutes with my second guest, George Montague, Speaker of the House of Commons. See you soon."

William Marshall is quickly alongside David and Sara. "That was marvellous television. Interesting, probing but always good-natured and polite. That is why we need you, Sara."

"I'm sorry about the last bit. David, you caught me off guard, but it was so nice of you to say that."

"Right, ninety seconds to air. David, thank you and goodbye. Sara, George Montague is in a foul mood."

"How can you tell?" asks David, laughing.

"If you feel he is going over the top then immediately go to an ad break. We'll be set up to do that at any point through the interview," Marshall tells Sara.

"Can I stay and watch this, please?" requests David McDougall.

"OK but keep well out of the way."

George Montague takes his place alongside Sara. He is grim-faced and silent.

"Hello again and welcome to the second part of today's programme. My guest now is Mr George Montague, Speaker of the House of Commons. Welcome, Mr Speaker. You have spoken out a lot recently about the need to uphold tradition both in Parliament and throughout the country. Could you please explain your concerns to the viewers?"

"Certainly. Parliament has traditions dating back hundreds of years. It is vital to preserve them in order to continue the discipline and status quo of our predecessors. Our successors expect us to hand over centuries of constancy when they inherit the responsibility. In 2034 the Dissolution of Parliament was delayed by six hours and overseen by the Deputy Prime Minister. I am still furious and embarrassed that, on my watch, such a flagrant breach of tradition took place. It was, of course, largely your fault."

Sara interrupts, "I don't remember that Dissolution. I was in hospital fighting for my life at the time."

"Quite so, but you had no business going to the Prime Minister's private quarters late at night just to have sex. I admit the PM made an error of judgement. Order and tradition were the losers, as usual."

"My hospital room was crammed with flowers and cards. My dressing room is the same today. One interesting thing I have noticed is that none of the good wishes I have received came from the Speaker's office or the House of Commons."

"Why would I send flowers to someone who, through greed and stupidity, nearly ruined a vital Parliamentary ceremony? You have no idea of the importance of tradition because you were born elsewhere. You do not belong here. You are not a true Briton. I am sure there are white males who could do your job better than you can, but it is the same old story these days. Equality. Every job goes to an immigrant, a woman or a homosexual."

Sara can hear William shouting in her ear, "Cut to a break now. Sara. Stop this now." At the back of the studio, a member of the crew is holding on to David to prevent him running down to the filming area.

The Speaker is continuing to rant, "You, of course, are all three plus a slut and a pervert."

Sara looks completely unruffled by the verbal onslaught and says calmly, "Do you not believe in equality? It is a very special word. So many people have had the opportunity to use their talents regardless of their background, age, sex or who they fall in love with. I agree it is not a white male world any longer. I think that is a marvellous thing. I get the feeling that you disagree with me. I am not white-skinned. I am a woman, and I am gay. Not much I can do about any of them, really. What would you do with me? Throw me in jail and add in some Godwin-style flogging and branding? Sentence me to death, maybe? Or deport me to where I came from and give my job to a heterosexual white male?"

"All three have merit, but I would have you deported if it was up to me."

"I, and many other people, are truly grateful that you aren't the person making the decisions."

"Order, discipline and doing things properly are what matters. People come from all over the world to see our traditional ceremonies like the Changing of the Guard, because they are historical and unchanging. That is the side of Britain we need to promote, not taking in any foreigner with a sob story. This country needs role models, not another sex-mad immigrant pervert. What kind of example are you giving to young women?"

"I came to England aged eighteen as a refugee. I went to university and worked hard to get where I am today. Surely, that is a good example for anyone. I cannot help who I fall in love with. You are more than welcome to come to my wedding. I will send you an invitation. If you come, you will see a normal wedding except there will be two brides. Everything else will be the same. The happy couple deeply in love, exchanging vows surrounded by the people who love them. Anyway, I think we have gone off the subject here. You are concerned that the monarchy is encroaching on Parliamentary territory. Could you elaborate on that, please?"

"Again, the problems started in 2034 with the Dissolution of Parliament. I was told that I could not explain the situation to Parliament until the King had addressed the nation. Totally unacceptable. There have been other incidents since then. I had to delay the State Opening of Parliament last year because the King was delayed. I run a tight ship. Parliament is always ready at the agreed time. I must say that I have no grievance at all with King Charles III. He is doing a splendid job, but the problem is an institutionalised desire to modernise and change. Some things should not be messed about with. Tradition, you see, is everything. How am I supposed to keep the old ways going for the next generation when the rest of the world is dashing headlong in the direction of whatever is the in thing this week? We are an ancient nation and I expect the mechanism around the monarchy to support me in upholding the old ways."

"Thank you, Mr Speaker, for explaining your views in such a forthright manner. I'm afraid that is all we have time for today. Thank you to my guests, David McDougall and George Montague. It has certainly been an interesting return to this programme for me. I hope you will tune in at the same time tomorrow. I will be here, providing I haven't been deported. Goodbye."

David McDougall rushes to Sara as soon as the programme finishes, closely followed by William Marshall. They say in unison, "Sara, are you alright?"

Before she can answer, George Montague departs the studio, looking even more grim-faced than when he arrived.

"I'm fine," Sara says. "I am sorry I ignored your ad break, but I guess I just wanted the last word. Six years ago, I would have probably burst into tears. Nowadays I am proud to be gay. I like myself and my sexuality is part of me. I can look after myself. David, I saw you trying to get down here but, both of you, I can handle people like Montague."

"That was wonderful. Ratings are through the roof apparently and they will all come back tomorrow," gushes William. "I need to find difficult guests for you, if you're going to carry on as you've started."

"Great. I would love to interview some of the

awkward brigade from the last few years. Nicola Sturgeon would be a challenge. Bring her on."

David speaks, "I am going to canvass support for a vote of no confidence in Montague. That was totally unacceptable. He's got to go."

*

It is nearly nine PM when a car approaches one of the many security barriers at Westminster. The guard approaches the driver.

"Oh, hello. My name is Nicolette Du Bois. Can I come through? I have a letter, well, an invitation, for Mr Montague. Or I suppose you could take it and give it to him."

"I'll let you through. I try to avoid him as much as possible."

Nic pulls up outside his accommodation and knocks on the door. Whilst waiting, she notices a crowd of people about four hundred metres away.

When George Montague opens the door, she says, "Hello, I'm Sara Molan's fiancée. Can I come in for a minute? I've brought your wedding invitation, but I would like a quick word."

Montague turns away and goes into his living room and sits down at his desk. Nic follows, walks up close to the Speaker and shoots him once in the head. As she does so, the sound of fireworks helps to mask the sound of the shot. Nic quickly arranges the scene to look like a suicide and lets herself out. She then puts the wedding invitation through the letterbox and goes back to her car.

"No reply," she tells the guard. "I expect he's at the firework display. What's that for?"

"I lose track of what they are celebrating. Centuries-old tradition, I expect."

*

Two hours later, CI Melville arrives at the scene to meet Sergeant Adams from the Downing Street police. "Tell me the worst."

"Well, sir. Mr Montague was last seen at eight PM when he talked to the professionals setting up the fireworks. People got a bit concerned when he didn't come out for the display. About ten, they told the police patrol and they entered with their master key. He was slumped across his desk with one bullet wound in his head. Appears to be suicide, but there is one odd thing. He had a visitor just before nine. Nicolette Du Bois. She told the guard she had an invitation to deliver. She drove in but was back in two or three minutes. She told the guard there was no answer. The invitation was sitting on the doormat when the patrol went in."

"So, death between eight and nine, if Nic was telling the truth."

"Surely, you don't think she killed him, sir?"

"First, Godwin and Nic and Sara just happened to be in Calais when he apparently killed himself. Now,

Montague and who is on the scene? Nic, delivering a wedding invitation. Two coincidences in a couple of months. Makes me suspicious."

"Are you taking over this one, then, sir?"

"Yes, I think I am. I might have to stand down from the case or the wedding, but that is up to Commissioner Giles. Have you been invited?"

"Yes sir. I've had an invitation. I was intending to go."

"I'll mention you as well to the Commissioner. I'll need your help for a while."

"Fine, sir. It will be nice to work with you again."

Despite being called out the previous night, Paul Melville is in his office before eight AM. He is soon joined by Sergeant Adams. Melville then speaks to Commissioner Giles.

"Ma'am, I was called out last night to the apparent suicide of the Speaker, George Montague. The cause of death is a single bullet wound to the head. Nicolette Du Bois visited him just before nine PM to deliver a wedding invitation. She posted the invite through the letterbox and told the guard on the gate that she could not get an answer from him."

"Have you spoken to her yet?"

"No, I am going to go round there shortly. There are a couple of other things, Ma'am. Firstly, is it alright if I borrow Sergeant Adams for a few days? He knows the current set-up at Westminster far better than I do and it would be helpful to have a witness when I talk to the ladies."

"Yes, that's fine. Tell his superior that I have authorised this."

"Thank you. The other problem is both Sergeant Adams and myself have been invited to the wedding ceremony for Sara Molan and Nicolette Du Bois. I think it would be useful for us to go but if you feel we should stay away then that's fine."

"I do not think that we can be sure a crime has been committed. I admit it is highly suspicious that one or both of them have been in the vicinity when two people they knew committed suicide. Unless you arrest one of them this morning, I am quite happy for you both to go. Please do not commit suicide and keep your eyes and ears open."

"Thank you, Ma'am. I will keep you up to date."

Turning to Sergeant Adams, he says, "The Commissioner is happy for me to borrow you for a few days, and she wants us to go to the wedding despite Montague. Come on. Let's see what Molan and Du Bois have to say for themselves."

*

"To what do we owe this pleasure?" asks Sara, cheerfully.

"I take it you haven't heard the news yet. George Montague was found dead last night at home. It looks like suicide, but it also looks like a duplicate of Bob Godwin's death. Oh, by the way, Sara, can I introduce

Sergeant Adams? You have met him, but you were unconscious and bleeding heavily at the time."

Sara lets out a scream and throws herself into the Sergeant's arms. When she has finished hugging and kissing him, Nic takes over.

Eventually, everyone settles down and Melville can continue, "Nic, it appears that you went to see him last night with a wedding invitation. Can you tell me what happened?"

"Well, not much really. Sara was determined to go ahead and invite him, even though he was so nasty to her on the programme. I said that he would just start shouting at her if she went, so I would go. I did ask the guard to deliver it, but he was not keen, so I drove to the Speaker's property. I knocked on the door but there was no answer. I tried the door, but it was locked. There was a firework display going on with a lot of people. I thought he was probably over there, but I didn't really like the idea of pushing through people watching the fireworks to find him. So, I posted the invitation through the letterbox and came home."

"Did you see anybody acting suspiciously?"

"No. The only people I saw were the ones watching the fireworks and they were about four or five hundred metres away."

"Sara, where were you?"

"Here, all night. Working on the wedding arrangements. I want a firework display now, but Nic isn't keen."

"Have you had any contact with George Montague since the programme?"

"No, I haven't. William Marshall might have done. He wanted the Speaker back on the show as quickly as possible. Rows and bigotry are very good for the ratings, you see."

"The George Montagues' of this world are a very, very small minority these days. The vast majority disagree with him completely."

"The problem for me is that it seems most members of that small minority are associated with British politics."

Sergeant Adams speaks for the first time. "Nic, are you sure the front door was locked?"

For a second, Nic looks puzzled by the question but replies firmly, "Yes. Definitely. I pushed it, but it was locked."

Sara asks, "What is happening about the investigation into Bob Godwin's death?"

CI Melville replies, "Nothing much. The French authorities have ruled it as a suicide. Unless any new evidence emerges, then that is how it will remain. A suicide. I imagine the same verdict will be brought in for the Speaker. He had been under tremendous pressure since your interview with the prospect of losing a vote of confidence and the widespread press coverage."

"You are making me feel guilty. There has been so much fuss about this. I was fine about it. He is entitled to his views even if they are non-PC and hopelessly out of date. I am truly sorry he found himself in a position where taking his own life seemed to be his only option."

"It is not your fault, Sara. Unless one of you pulled the trigger, then you are not to blame. Let's talk about something nicer. How are the wedding plans going?"

"Not too bad. Late nights and early mornings but we're getting there. Only three weeks to go, I hope you are both still coming."

Sergeant Adams replies, "Yes, we both are. Really looking forward to it."

Sara says, "You are more than welcome to stay and talk to Nic. But I must start getting ready to go to work. The Sewage Minister and the Leader of the House this morning. I can hardly contain my excitement."

CI Melville responds, "We came in case Nic had any information, so we are done. Thank you for your time."

After the policemen leave, Nic and Sara kiss. "Well done, Nic. Ice cool as always. I know it's early but let's have a drink to the memory of George Montague. How about a toast to a racist, sexist bastard, formerly of the parish of Westminster?"

"Fine by me. I'll get the glasses. Anyone else you want to be rid of?"

"Not at the moment. I think we should lay low for a bit. Melville's no fool. He can place one or both of us near the scene of both deaths. We don't want to pile up too many coincidences now, do we?"

*

On their way back to Westminster police station CI Melville and Sergeant Adams discuss the interview.

Melville asks, "Why did you ask her about being sure the door was locked?"

"I thought it might unnerve her and I think it did. For a second, she was wondering if she had made a mistake and left the door open,"

"Yes, I noticed that. You think she killed Montague, don't you?"

"Let's say I have reasonable doubt. Added to their presence in Calais as well, it all appears very suspicious. I must say that they are very cool customers, and it is going to be very hard to prove. They've got their stories straight and that's that."

"I am sure they killed Godwin and Montague. But I think it is more likely that the proof is going to come from France. I want Claude Abbeye to look more closely at what they got up to in Paris for five years. Can you go back to the Speaker's property? Take some constables with you and see if you can find the door key. If we are right then Nic took the key from Montague, locked the door behind her and left. I think it is unlikely she would dump it nearby, but you never know and there might be fingerprints somewhere nearby too."

*

Later that morning, Melville rings Claude Abbeye.

"Bonjour, Claude. There has been a development

here last night and I need your help. Recently Sara Molan had a row with one of the guests on her programme. That gentleman, the Speaker of the House of Commons, committed suicide last night with a single bullet to the head. Sound familiar?"

"Oui. Definitely. Any connection other than the row?"

"Montague, the Speaker, died between eight PM and ten PM. At roughly nine PM, Nicolette Du Bois visited his house to deliver a wedding invitation. Her story is that she knocked on the door but got no answer. She tried the handle but claims the door was locked. She posted the invitation through the door and left. There was an envelope containing the invitation on the mat when police entered the property."

"It seems strange that you invite someone you had an argument with to your wedding."

"Actually, that fits in. On the programme, Sara invited him after he called her a pervert for marrying another woman. Told him that, if he came, he would see just another marriage ceremony but with two brides. They claim they were just honouring Sara's promise. I would say the invitation provided the perfect excuse for Nic going there."

"Any forensics?"

"None so far. Also, there was a fireworks display taking place nearby. Nobody saw anything except coloured smoke in the sky and, more importantly, nobody heard a shot."

"They are either incredibly clever or very lucky."

"I think that Nic is the clever one. In many ways, she has perfected a brilliant MO. Certainly, both Godwin and Montague were obvious candidates to take their own lives. A bit of manipulation of the scene to fit a suicide scenario and a plausible story for being in the area if the police come calling. I guess we've both got one body apiece now. Would you be able to do some digging for me? She must have done this before Godwin. Can you get the relevant forces to check whether they had any similar suicides? I'm interested in Paris between 2020 and 2026; and 2029 to 2031. Then Lyon 2030 to 2032 and finally Marseilles for the years 2031 to 2034. There is a bit of overlap in the years because I am not sure exactly when she moved. I know it is a lot of work for a hunch, but if there are any matching cases, we might be able to tie her in somehow. We're not getting away work-free. I'll get my Sergeant to check out London for the years she was living with Sara Molan here."

"I've got all that. Just don't expect an answer tomorrow morning."

*

The next day, Sergeant Adams enters CI Melville's office.

"No sign of the key and there are no usable fingerprints anywhere."

"Pity. If we could prove she was inside, we just might have the start of a case. Next job for you is to check the records for London from 2026 to 2029. You are looking for any suicide with a single shot to the head with everything arranged just right for a self-inflicted shot. If you find any, see if you can find a link to Sara and Nic. I have no idea what work is involved but you can get PC Hellier to help you, if necessary. Claude is doing the same for Paris, Lyon and Marseilles."

"Sir, I do find it a bit hard to see Nic as a serial killer. She's just too nice. I think she may have topped Montague to avenge Sara, but I find it hard to see her as an international gun for hire."

"I don't think the motive is money. At the moment it seems to be revenge on people who betrayed Sara. We need to think about who else has upset her over the years and if anyone else is in danger."

"William Marshall let Sara down when she visited Godwin. Should I give him a heads-up?"

"No, not yet. He'll either tell Molan or start acting so strangely that she guesses something is going on. I think he is reasonably safe, as he is Sara's boss, and she has something on him. I'm hoping he gets pissed at the wedding and blurts out his secret. I would bet on some kind of sleazy sex scandal. I will get him, but at the moment let's concentrate on our two main suspects."

CHAPTER 6

THE TWO BRIDES

September 2040

Nic wakes up at six fifteen on her wedding morning. She automatically reaches across the bed for Sara, but she is not there. A momentary panic soon subsides when she realises that her fiancée is staying at the wedding venue in Greenwich. They are both staying there after the ceremony– the nearest they can manage to a honeymoon with Sara's work commitments. Despite the early hour, Nic gets up, showers and has a slice of dry toast for breakfast. During the morning, people come and go. The hairdresser puts Nic's hair up and the make-up artist works on making her face shine. The next ring on the doorbell produces two giggling bridesmaids known professionally as Kerri and Amie. They are more interested in any alcohol around than in Nic's attempts to get them to try on their bridesmaids' outfits. Eventually, and with probably a couple of glasses of wine too many inside them, the girls agree to get ready.

"I hope your measurements were accurate because there is nothing I can do now if they don't fit," says Nic, as her bridesmaids disappear into the spare bedroom.

Thirty minutes later, they emerge, each wearing black stilettos, black tights, white skirts finishing a little above the knee and brown silk blouses.

"You look magnificent," exclaims Nic. "Keep the blouses buttoned up to the neck during the ceremony. At the reception, you can undo as many buttons as you like." Nic then disappears to put on her own wedding outfit.

Another thirty minutes passes before she reappears. The girls have made good use of the time, emptying another bottle of wine between them. When they first see Nic, they both stare open-mouthed for a few seconds before bursting into applause. Nic is wearing white court shoes and a dress stopping just above her knees. The top half of the dress is white, and the bottom brown. Time is moving on and there is only time for one quick drink before the wedding cars arrive.

*

Sara wakes up at seven thirty, well rested after a good night's sleep in the venue's wedding suite. She has a leisurely breakfast in the dining room before returning to her room. She has borrowed the hairdresser and make-up expert from her television programme. It takes over two hours' work before Sara is satisfied with the mass of curls hairstyle and her make-up. The manicurist is next and has only just left when David McDougall arrives.

"It can't be that time already," Sara shrieks. "I'm not even dressed yet."

"You look gorgeous, but it is probably better if you don't marry in jeans. It's two o'clock, so you've got thirty minutes. Nic will be on her way any minute now."

"Aargh," gasps Sara as she dashes into the bedroom.

Twenty-eight minutes later, she re-emerges to a "Wow. You look incredible," from David. Sara is dressed identically to Nic, except that the colours are reversed on the dress, with brown at the top and white for the bottom half.

Sara asks, "Will I do?"

David replies, "You look a million dollars. You will more than do. You'll knock them dead. Who's supposed to be early and who's supposed to be late?"

"I'm already here, so I have to be on time at least."

"We've got thirty seconds, then."

As David and Sara enter the wedding room and become visible to the guests, there is a collective gasp from the guests at the beauty and simplicity of the bride and her outfit. They sit down at the front on the right-hand side. Five minutes later, the guests rise, quickly followed by Sara and David, as Nic, Kerri and Amie enter to "Here Comes the Bride" and make their somewhat less-than-stately passage to the front of the room, taking their places on the left-hand side. The registrar asks the brides to come forward.

"We are gathered here today to witness the joining together in matrimony of Sara Louise Molan and Nicolette Du Bois. The two brides have asked me to thank you all for coming today and to thank you for your support during several difficult years for them. I must ask the following question. Is there anyone present who knows of any just cause or impediment why the couple before us should not be joined together by marriage here today?" An uneasy silence descends but to everyone's relief no objections are made. The registrar continues, "Sara and Nicolette have written their own vows which I will now ask them to read."

Melville whispers to Adams. "Sara Louise, as in Louise Land." The sergeant nods in agreement.

Sara turns to Nic and starts speaking. "Nic, I love you now and will do so throughout eternity. We have faced difficulties that have nearly destroyed me, but your strength has brought me safely to this happy place today in front of the people we think the most of. I vow to love you forever. I vow to stay with you and share this journey with you wherever it may take us. I vow to be faithful and to give my love only to you, Nic. I give you my hand and this ring (David McDougall steps forward at this point and hands over a gold wedding band) as my contribution to our lifelong unbroken circle."

Sara whispers, "I love you, Nic."

The first reaction is two loud screams of approval from Kerri and Amie, which earns them a glare from the registrar.

Nic speaks next, "Sara, I promise to be with you until death separates us. I love you with all my heart and I give my heart to you today, tomorrow and always. You are my whole life, my everything. I promise to be faithful, to be a good wife to you and to keep no secrets from you throughout our lives together, Sara, je t'aimerai pour toujours. I give you this ring." There is a delay at this point as the bridesmaids try to find the ring. This is eventually found inside Amie's bra and duly handed over to Nic. "I give you this ring as my contribution to our ongoing unbroken circle."

Several of the female guests are in tears by the end of Nic's vows and the bridesmaids are no exception.

The registrar takes the two rings and hands Sara's ring to Nic and Nic's ring to Sara, saying, "These rings represent the circle Sara and Nic are forming today through their vows and this ceremony of marriage. By the powers invested in me as a registrar, I pronounce you wife and wife, joined together in matrimony. You may kiss."

As the happy couple kiss, the guests rise and clap or cheer, in the case of Kerri and Amie.

The registrar says, "The newlyweds invite all their guests to join them in the dining room opposite for the reception. If you will all follow the happy couple out of the wedding room and make your way into the dining room, the newlyweds will join you very soon."

The guests do as they are told and find themselves in an enormous room, well stocked with a superb-looking buffet, a free bar and a six-piece band on a stage at the far end of the room. Immediately in front of the stage is a small dance floor. Mrs Melville says quietly to her husband, "No expense spared here." He replies, "Makes me think I should be a TV presenter."

The band suddenly springs into life, playing "Here Comes the Bride" as Sara and Nic enter the dining room, arm in arm. They are still in their wedding outfits and look serene and incredibly happy. At first people are reluctant to eat or drink, but once a brave guest approaches the buffet, a queue soon forms. The Melvilles and Sergeant Adams soon join the fray.

"This is amazing," says the Sergeant, looking at the array of food, which is dominated by a whole salmon swimming in blue ice. The guests can choose between Indian, French, vegetarian and vegan selections plus various cold meats, although no ham is on show. "This must have cost a packet," continues Adams.

The Chief Inspector replies, "But where is the money coming from? They've only been back three months and, as far as I know, only Sara is working."

"Will they change their names?" Mrs Melville asks.

"I have no idea," replies her husband. As he speaks, he sees Nic heading towards them in the food queue.

"Congratulations," CI Melville says, and this is quickly echoed by the other two. "My wife has a question for you."

Mrs Melville looks uncomfortable, but asks Nic, "Are you keeping your own surnames or changing to Molan-Du Bois?"

"Non. We are staying just as we are. Nicolette Du Bois and Sara Molan. What did you think of the ceremony?"

"Very emotional. I cried during the vows. It was all so beautiful."

As Mrs Melville speaks, raised voices can be heard from the other side of the room. It quickly becomes clear that Sara and William Marshall are having a disagreement. Nic goes to calm troubled waters and peace is soon restored. Soon after, the band starts up and the brides take to the dance floor for the first dance. Most of the guests, including the Melvilles, follow Sara and Nic on to the dance floor. Very few notice Marshall and his partner, a young slim redhead, exiting the venue. Outside, nobody sees Marshall hand cash to the girl and drive off alone, with a malicious grin on his face.

The party continues with Kerri and Amie inadvertently providing great entertainment with their antics. Some are funny, like Kerri unbuttoning her blouse completely and Amie showing several bewildered male guests exactly where she hid the ring. Other tricks are not quite so well received. Sara objects strongly to finding meat in the vegetarian section of the buffet and Kerri's topless dancing is unlikely to make the final cut of the wedding video. Soon after that, Nic gathers up her rowdy bridesmaids and the three of them leave together with the drunken pair loudly singing "Here Comes the Bride" and "Agadoo.".

Mrs Melville has had enough by about ten o'clock, but her husband is not keen to leave until Nic returns. She comes back about two hours after departing. After a brief chat to Sara, the happy couple return to the dancing area, cutting shapes gymnastically. The Melvilles and Sergeant Adams leave soon after, shouting their congratulations and goodbyes to the gyrating newlyweds.

*

Despite the eating, drinking and frivolity of the previous night, CI Melville is at his desk at nine o'clock promptly. Within seconds, his phone rings.

"Hello, sir. I am Inspector Madden. I am at a crime scene I think you might be interested in at Tooting, sir."

For Melville, walking into the terraced property in Tooting is a case of déjà vu. A dead male slumped over his office desk with one bullet hole in his head and a gun lying on the floor nearby.

"Have you identified him? If not, I know who he is."

Inspector Madden replies, "Well, we have found papers in the name of William Marshall but no passport or driver's licence on him."

"Yes, that is the body of William Marshall. He was a television producer and I spent yesterday afternoon and early evening with him at a wedding reception.

He seemed to have a row of some kind with one of the brides and then left, about eight I would say."

"Alone?"

"No. He left with a woman. Red hair, small, late teens or early twenties. Any sign of her?"

"None. Lucky girl. If she had come home with him, she would probably be dead too. There is a Mrs Marshall. We have spoken to her. She is at her mother's in Dunstable, Kent. She is coming back. She has been caring for her sick mother and was coming back today, anyway."

"Any suicide note?"

"We haven't found one. We are still looking. The only thing we have found of interest is some dirty photos. Same girl in all of them."

"Let me guess. Young, small with red hair. Can you e-mail me one or two of the milder ones? I will ask my wife and Sergeant Adams if it is the same girl who was at the wedding with him. Ask Mrs Marshall if she knows who her husband was taking with him yesterday?"

"Are you taking this on, sir?"

"No, I am quite happy for you to handle this. Let me know exactly what Mrs Marshall has to say and I would like a copy of your final report. I am, however, going to interview the happy couple from the wedding yesterday."

"They will be on the other side of the world by now," states Inspector Madden.

"Not these two. Staying at the wedding venue

for a day or two and then relaxing at home together, apparently. Ring me if you find out who the girl is."

"Do you think she is important?"

"Probably not, but I would dearly like to know whether she was here when Marshall died and if she saw anything. Do you have a time of death?"

"Between eight and midnight last night. Are we treating it as suicide?"

CI Melville smiles wryly as he says, "The victim was murdered but evidence of that is non-existent, so at present, it is another suicide like Montague and Godwin. Maybe one day they will get the justice they deserve."

*

The Chief Inspector's next stop is at the Greenwich wedding venue. By now, it is ten thirty AM. He finds the suite and knocks several times before the door is answered by a tired, looking Sara Molan, with a dressing gown wrapped around her body.

"Sorry," she says, wearily. "We're still in bed. It was a long day and a busy night." She laughs but looking at Melville's solemn expression, she adds, "Look, come in. Has something happened?"

Once inside, CI Melville asks, "Can you get Nic out here too, please?"

Sara disappears into the bedroom and returns a few minutes later with a yawning Nic. Like her wife, Nic is wearing a dressing gown. They offer the Chief Inspector a drink, which he refuses, and sit on the settee holding hands as he starts to speak.

"I was called this morning to a property in Tooting, where police had discovered the body of one of your wedding guests."

Both women look shocked and Sara gasps, "Please no. Not David."

"Why would you think it was Mr McDougall?"

"Because he has been getting death threats ever since he started the vote of no confidence against George Montague."

"I will get someone to look into that, but it isn't him. It is William Marshall. Looks like suicide. Exactly the same as Bob Godwin and George Montague."

Sara begins to weep and is comforted by Nic. After some hugging and reassuring words, Sara responds, "This is terrible. Why would he kill himself? The show is booming. So many people close to us committing suicide. Why?"

"I am hoping you can tell me that. You told me you knew why Godwin was blackmailing Marshall. Time to reveal the secret, Sara."

"William was having an affair, which was bad enough, but apparently when they started his girlfriend was thirteen years old."

"What do you know about the girl?"

"She was described to me as little, redheaded and called Suzi."

"Just like the girl with Marshall at your wedding. I heard you arguing with him until Nic calmed things down."

"Oh, that was nothing," interjects Nic.

"It didn't look like nothing to me. Now, we can do this civilly here or we can do this formally at the station. The truth, please."

"Alright," says Sara. "I just flipped when I saw that he had brought his bit on the side to my wedding. I almost died because of his libido. I did not want to be reminded of it on the happiest day of my life. We exchanged words, I admit, but that was all. Over and forgotten as quickly as it began."

"Did you tell him to leave?"

"No. Nic and I led the first dance straight after and when we eventually came off the floor, he had disappeared along with that trollop."

"Did you invite his wife?"

"Yes, and I understood she was coming. That was another reason why I got annoyed."

"It appears that Mrs Marshall was called away to care for her sick mother. I've asked the Inspector in charge of the case to ask her who was supposed to be going in her place. We are anxious to find the girl. There is no trace of her at Marshall's house, so we need to make sure she is safe. Nic, why were you missing from your own reception for the best part of two hours?"

"I was sorting out the bridesmaids, otherwise known as The Chuckle Sisters. They were, how do you say, pissed as a judge." Sara and Melville both laugh but make no attempt to correct her. "It is quite a drive from here to our house. Then they took ages to get changed. I mean, how long does it take to take off one set of clothes and put on your own jeans and top? They were still paralytic so no taxi would take them in that state, so I had to take them to the nearest Tube station and get them on a Northern Line train. I just hope they got off at Camden Town. They probably spent the night asleep going up and down the Northern Line. I would probably have missed everything if I had driven to Camden."

"You went to the wedding in a limousine. Whose car did you drive?"

"Mine, of course," replies Sara. "And before you ask, she is fully insured to drive it."

"Do either of you know where Marshall lives?"

"No." They both reply.

"You are known to, or have a connection with, three people who have all committed suicide in the last few months in identical circumstances. If you know anything at all about what is going on, then you need to tell me now. Can you think of anyone who might be trying to help you or avenge you by eliminating people who hurt you, Sara, in some way?"

Nic replies, "Do you think Sara is in any danger?"

"I don't know. It is hard to know whether they are genuine suicides or murders. All three victims had problems in their lives, but troubled individuals end their lives in a variety of ways. For three people who are connected to each other to die in a relatively short term in identical ways is extremely unusual. The connection is Sara. That leads me to think that either you two are behind all this or you could be future targets."

"We know nothing about this. I don't have any crazy fans stalking me or sending me marriage proposals. I am certainly not a murderer, and I am not married to one either," says Sara, emotionally.

"Do we need protection?" asks Nic.

"In the short term, I can assign an officer to protect you but police finances are tight as usual, so I think you may need to consider paying for long-term protection yourselves."

Nic replies, "I think we need to be safe, Sara. If these are murders made to look like suicide, then one or both of us could be next. I'm scared."

Sara hugs her wife and then says, "Can we have an officer outside the apartment for a few days? I am off work for a few more days, so we will not be going out much. We will look seriously at getting bodyguards for the future."

"I can do two weeks maximum, but once you are back at work and moving around more, then it will be down to you, I'm afraid. I will arrange something as soon as I get back to the office."

"Thank you very much. Right, Nic and I are going back to bed."

"Would you care to join us, Chief Inspector?" Nic asks straight-faced. "You might learn something." She laughs heartily.

Paul Melville blushes, makes his excuses and goes back to the office.

CHAPTER 7

NATALIE

September 2040

Having eventually persuaded Commissioner Giles that it was worth the expense of providing security for Sara and Nic for two weeks to keep an eye on them and hopefully prevent more deaths, Melville decides it is time to speak to Claude Abbeye again.

"Chief Inspector. I was going to ring you today. I have some interesting but worrying information for you. But you tell me your news first."

"Over here, we have another identical suicide. Same MO as Godwin and Montague. The victim is, or was, William Marshall, a TV boss and executive producer of Sara Molan's programme."

"What do they have to say about it?"

"Complete surprise. Nic and Sara got married yesterday and I attended the wedding. The deceased had a row with Sara Molan. According to her, she got upset because Marshall brought his mistress to the ceremony instead of his wife. He left, with his partner, soon afterwards. The girlfriend has disappeared, and we don't know if she is involved, kidnapped, dead or just hiding. The problem for me is that Nic disappeared later with two drunken bridesmaids. The story is that she drove them back to her place to change out of their wedding outfits. That took ages, apparently, and then she drove them to a Northern Line tube station and put them on the train. After that, she drove back to the reception. In theory, it checks out, just about. The bridesmaids were totally out of it and I can easily imagine them taking ages to do any simple task. The happy couple claim to be scared. The way they are selling it is that if these are murders, then someone unknown to them is killing off their associates one by one and they could be next. I've assigned an officer to them for two weeks, so we can keep an eye on them and pray there aren't any more suicides in the next fortnight."

"As usual, only circumstantial evidence. If they are guilty, then they are really calm and unflappable."

"I know that they are lying but they are so damn good at it that I am beginning to have doubts."

"Now," says Claude. "I have some stories to tell you. I will send you the relevant files, but I think I should talk you through it all and see what you think is relevant. Paris police sent me the details of this one, which goes back to 2020. A woman named Madame Charambeaux complained to police that her next door neighbour, a Monsieur Frederic Anson, had raped her fourteen-year-old daughter. Anson denied everything and the girl refused to even speak to the police. In the end, they had no choice but to drop the matter. The community, however, turned on Anson. He lost his job and his neighbours shunned him. About two weeks after the investigation was closed, he was found dead with a single bullet hole in his head. An obvious suicide. His wife insisted he was not suicidal and that he had never owned a gun, but it was ruled to be suicide and that was that. The Paris police have really helped us. They went back to the neighbourhood and found a couple of people there who remembered M. Anson. They say that he was not the type to rape anyone or cheat on his wife. They recalled that the girl, Bernice Charambeaux, was wild and had a string of boyfriends. She was beautiful and had long black hair. Can you see anything familiar about this?"

"How old was Anson?"

"Just a second, er, oh, here it is. Forty-five."

"Nic told me she lost her virginity when she was fourteen and seduced her forty-five-year-old neighbour. The letters n-i-c appear in her first name, the description fits and, of course, the MO is an exact replica of what we have been seeing in the last few months. I am speculating here but if she told me the truth, then she seduced Anson. He was getting all sorts of grief about it all, so suppose he decided to tell the police exactly what happened. Nic didn't want that. They argued and she shot him and made it look like suicide."

"An excellent theory but nothing more than that. As always with this case, it is all circumstantial. We cannot prove that Anson was murdered and if he was, anyone could have killed him. His wife, an angry local or even Bernice's parents."

"I agree but I think that one fits perfectly, so let's claim that file for the time being."

"Certainement. Case number two. Paris 2023. Police found a criminal named Charles Souvet dead in his apartment. He had been shot once in the head and the gun used was nearby. Souvet was left-handed. He had been shot on the left side and the gun had fallen to the left. He had a lengthy criminal record for assault, control of prostitutes and drug dealing. Neighbours said that there had been a girl living there for about five weeks. Young, slim, very pretty and black hair. She had been seen going out at night, sometimes alone but usually with Souvet, wearing very little. There was some evidence of a female presence – a few clothes and make-up in the bathroom but no match for fingerprints. Police never traced her. It was ruled a suicide with the proviso that the case would be re-opened if his girlfriend was traced and had important new evidence. As far as the police were concerned, if someone did kill him then they deserved a medal. Interested?"

"Yes, I am. Except for Anson all the victims were nasty characters, who are unlikely to be missed by many people. If it was Nic, then she must have been attacked or threatened in some way to react like that. The current cases seem to be aimed at protecting Sara Molan but in these earlier incidents she seems to be looking after herself. Another case for us to sit on, I think."

"Bien. Now number three is different, so see what you think. In 2025, a police patrol noticed a valuable car parked in a deserted industrial estate about one kilometre from any form of civilisation. They found a body in the driver's seat with one shot to the head and the gun lying nearby in the car. His wallet was in his jacket, but all identification, cards and cash were taken. The cards were never used. The vehicle was a Lamborghini, and it was traced to a M Phillippe Grasset, a twenty-five-year-old stockbroker. He was earning big money and spending it as well. His live-in girlfriend said he often went out alone at night to meet colleagues and friends. It was not unusual for him to stay out all night. He had no work problems and was just about solvent despite his lavish spending. He was twice the drink driving limit and had cocaine in his bloodstream. Police found a couple of prostitutes who knew Grasset well. He was, apparently, a regular user of call girls. One thought she had seen him that night talking to a fairly new girl called Nicky. She was described as young, slim with black hair. She was never traced. Unusually, the verdict here was given as an unsolved death. The thinking was that, although it looked like a suicide there was some evidence that he may have had a passenger when he drove into the industrial site. If so, then it was just possible that the passenger killed him and took his money and cards."

"It almost fits, doesn't it? Killing method is the same and it sounds like Nic but stealing from his wallet and the outside scene are quite different. That was in 2025 and Nic was over here by 2026 at the latest. She may have fled France to avoid arrest for killing Grasset, I suppose. Let's put that one in a maybe pile at the moment."

"The next possible case is in Paris in 2030. The body of a man in his late fifties was found in a park. He had a single bullet wound to the head. A gun was found nearby. At first, it was treated as suicide but then his widow, Mme Benoit, told police that he was visiting his mistress at an apartment about three hundred metres from the park. According to Mme Benoit, her husband was fed up with the woman and intended to end the relationship. Police went to the flat. There were many personal items and pieces of furniture there but no tenant. Neighbours said that a young woman had lived there for about a year. She had several gentleman callers. One would call regularly for a few months and then disappear, to be replaced by a different man. Rent records showed the property was let to Veronica Tallon. Fingerprints were taken from the flat, but no match was found. I did enquire about matching them with the prints from the Souvet case but, unfortunately, both sets have been destroyed. No description this time and another outside death site."

"Nic told me that when she split from Sara in 2029, she went back to Paris but struggled to find modelling work. She needed to pay the rent, so she became the mistress of a man who paid her rent and gave her gifts in return for having sex with her whenever he wished. I think there was more than one man, but never at the same time apparently. She left Paris in either late 2030 or early 2031. It would explain her move to Lyon. It seems very risky to kill someone in a public park and so near to her address. On the other hand, she probably left the flat in a hurry, leaving some of her stuff behind. I think it is unlikely that we are going to find new evidence on that one, so another maybe I think."

"You will be pleased to know that there is only one case left but it is a beauty. Natalie Jamin."

"Never heard of her."

"If you were a French police officer, you would have. It is a famous case. Jamin worked for a casino in Lyon as head of the cash office. She was responsible for checking the amount of money handed in by individual croupiers with their receipt and expenditure records. She simply took money out and altered the records accordingly. It is believed she did this for the whole twelve years she was in that role. She was only caught, in early 2031, after an anonymous phone call from a woman who said that Jamin had told her what she was doing. She was arrested at work and police then went to her flat almost immediately. They found very little. Jamin's clothes and some very tired pieces of furniture. No evidence of spending and also no evidence of anyone else living there. And no cash at all. Jamin was charged with stealing five hundred thousand Euro because the casino only kept records for twelve months. If she had been stealing at that level for twelve years, she could have netted six million Euro. Estimates of how much she stole vary between three million Euro and ten million Euro. She pleaded guilty and was jailed for five years and ordered to repay five hundred thousand Euro or face a further five years in jail. Now, this is where it gets interesting. In late 2033, Jamin went to the appeal court seeking early release. Her lawyer argued that, in order to repay the five hundred thousand Euro, she needed to be out of prison to track down the stolen funds. The judge must have been out of her mind, but she agreed and Jamin was released from prison for three months. If she repaid the money owed within the three months and handed over any surplus cash, she could stay free. If she did not pay back the money due then she would go back to prison and serve an additional eight years instead of the five originally handed down. She was not allowed to leave her probation hostel without a police officer accompanying her or to leave Lyon without the court's permission. Everything went well for the first two months but in February 2034, Jamin suddenly disappeared from Lyon. Two days later, her body was found lying in the driveway of an industrial estate five kilometres from the centre of Marseilles. She had been killed by a single shot to the head and a gun was lying nearby. At first it looked like a straightforward suicide but soon questions began to be asked. How did Jamin get to the industrial estate? She had no vehicle in Marseilles and enquiries showed that no taxi had taken her there. Somebody must have driven her there and could, quite conceivably, have killed her. Why did Jamin risk jail by leaving Lyon? Where is the money? These unsolved problems led to the death being treated as murder. The file is open, and the investigation continues. Are you interested?"

"Very much so. My theory is that Nic either tipped off the casino and stole the money or Jamin realised she was about to be caught and asked Nic to look after the money. Nic told me she lived with a woman who went to prison for stealing from her employer, but she insisted she had nothing to do with the thefts. Nik moved to Marseilles in 2031 and told me she lived like a nun. But even nuns have expenses. Jamin gets out of jail and wants her money. Somehow she tracks Nic to Marseilles and demands however many million Euros she stole. Nic says "Fine" but it is hidden in Marseilles and I am not risking bringing it to Lyon, so you must come to Marseilles. When Jamin arrives, Nic tells her the money is hidden at an industrial estate and they must collect it at night. Du Bois drives her there, shoots her, makes it look like suicide in her normal way and drives off, leaving the body to be discovered the next day. By 2034, Nic was back in contact with Sara. I would guess that Nic was ecstatic when Molan asked for her help to escape Godwin's clutches. The plan was probably to use the favour done that night as leverage for them to get back together and allow Nic to flee to London. She must have thought all her birthdays had come at once when I rang up and told her Sara had been stabbed. She was able to get away from the police investigation in Marseilles, presumably with the money, and play the devoted ex sitting by Sara's bedside until she woke up. As soon as that happened, they were back together and engaged."

"You are almost certainly correct but once again it is entirely circumstantial."

"I know. I think we are going to have to play a long game here. We need to get concrete evidence before we can do anything."

"Do you want me to tell Marseilles our theory?"

"Yes, but stress to them that we need firm evidence, and it may be months or even years before that happens."

"I will keep in touch."

Melville then rings Sergeant Adams.

"Have you had any luck with the old cases?"

"Not really, sir. Nothing stands out so far."

"Don't do any more work on it for the time being. Claude has come up with some interesting possibilities, so I think the best way forward is to concentrate on them."

The next call is to David McDougall. "Sara Molan mentioned to me that you had received death threats. Do you want protection or are there any threats you feel particularly concerned about and would like us to investigate?"

"Chief Inspector, as an opposition MP, threats are an occupational hazard. I have upset the hard line traditionalists over George Montague, but they are no danger. Thank you for the offer but I will soldier on at present."

"Three people connected to Sara Molan have committed suicide this year. If a third party is connected with these deaths in any way at all, then you need to be extremely careful. Sara and Nic are worried and have accepted a police guard on their property. If you change your mind, please let me know."

No sooner has CI Melville finished this call than his phone rings and he is speaking to Inspector Madden.

"I am at the victim's house. Mrs Marshall has returned home. She wants to talk to you in person about two separate matters, she says."

"Fine. Have you got a spare officer who could drive her to Westminster police station?"

"Yes, we can do that."

"Excellent. I will talk to her here then."

CHAPTER 8

ELIZABETH AND LINDA

September 2040

Elizabeth Marshall duly arrives and takes a seat in CI Melville's office.

"Firstly, I wish to offer my deepest sympathy for your tragic loss. I expect Inspector Madden has told you that we are looking for the young woman who accompanied your husband to the wedding of Sara Molan and Nicolette Du Bois. Do you have any idea who your husband was planning to take with him in your absence?"

"He told me he was not going. If you want to find any of his female friends, I suggest you try King's Cross after dark."

"The girl is young, slim and has red hair. She might be called Suzi."

"Whoever she is, she is definitely not Suzi. She was

my husband's great hope. I actually thought he was going to leave me for her. She told him she was sixteen when they first met. When he found out she had been thirteen at the start of his rooting, he dropped her instantly. In early 2034, she was killed in a car crash. Her latest sugar daddy was killed too. We went to her funeral."

"Would you know her full name?"

"Suzanne McDougall."

"It's a common name but was she related to the MP David McDougall?"

"He was her father by his first wife, but he had little to do with her."

"Did he know about your husband's affair with his underage daughter?"

"William thought he did, but nothing was ever said publicly. It all became immaterial when she died."

"Your husband took a lookalike to the wedding, presumably to upset Sara Molan. It worked. They had quite a row at the reception. How were things between him and Sara?"

"Terrible. Since she came back to the show, ratings have rocketed. She seems to think it is entirely down to her. She has been playing the diva card. She even wrote to the Managing Director to get the right to choose her own guests. William was furious. She wanted to bring in non-political people and anyone who could be attached to an ethnic, sexual or gender minority. William wanted her out, but, of course, the ratings take precedence over everything."

"Were you aware of your husband's other friends like Suzi?"

"Some of them. The ones who lasted more than a couple of quickies. Freda lasted about a year. Tamara was another with staying power. There were so many who just came and then went."

"Do you know if he had a personal relationship with Sara Molan?"

"He tried when she was around the first time, but he never got anywhere. Of course, when she hit the headlines for being stabbed, it all came out. Poor William, he was built totally wrong for Ms Molan's sensibilities."

"I don't know if you can answer this, but Sara claimed she used Suzi to blackmail your husband to take her back. Why was he still afraid of the story if Suzi is dead?"

"I would say that was a lie. William contacted Sara. At the time, he needed her. Ratings were falling and in six years he could not find even one half-decent presenter. If she did threaten to go public on Suzi, he would have laughed and told her to go ahead."

"Do you know anyone who would want to kill your husband?"

"Sara Molan. Inspector Madden told me it was suicide."

"It probably is, but there have been several high-profile suicides recently, so we are investigating thoroughly. Inspector Madden will file a report and I have little doubt it will say suicide."

"William would never have killed himself. Not in his character to do something like that. Besides, he swore he would always look after me even after his death. He had this insurance policy paying me a lot of money on his death. I will get nothing if it is suicide."

"How much is a lot of money?"

"Two million pounds."

"Wow. Have you noticed anything unusual, however minor, in the last few weeks?"

"Well, there were a couple of things. Sara asked William to hire Nic as her personal assistant. He said that there were more than enough people already running around after her, but she could use Nic if she paid for the help herself. A few days later, Sara told him to forget about it. They had come up with a better idea."

"Strange. Mm. What was the other matter?"

"William had found a new girlfriend. She is called Diana Sheriff. Works at the TV studio. William rarely played that close to his work, but actually this one was better than most. Very pretty, but she had brains as well. She's an executive and clever. I actually liked her. Anyway, he brought her to the house to meet me. We had just had the wedding invitation and she saw it. There was a photograph of the happy couple on the front. She insisted that she recognised Nic. But she did not recognise the name. It was driving her mad trying to remember where she had seen Nic before."

"Thank you. I will talk to Ms Sheriff about that. In the meantime, if there is anything at all I can do to help, just let me know. I will find someone to drive you home."

*

Pressure of work keeps CI Melville busy, and it is a week later before he finds time to talk to Diana Sheriff in her work cubicle.

"I have been talking to Elizabeth Marshall."

"Yes, well, I can imagine what she said about me."

"Actually, she was complimentary. Said you were very pretty and clever. Did William Marshall ever give you any indication of taking his own life?"

"No. He had a zest for life. I cannot believe it."

"Did he mention any problems or enemies or threats?"

"William's working and private lives were one long problem. He was effectively doing two jobs. He oversaw all non-fiction programming, and he was executive producer for Sara Molan's show. He had been moaning about her recently. She was trying to take control of the whole shebang. She wanted to choose her own guests, pick her own team and widen the type of guests beyond political figures. I think he agreed with some of the plans, but he hated that she was trying to oust him. As for enemies – Sara Molan, Sara Molan and Sara Molan. He didn't talk to me about threats, but I am sure he must have got some, particularly after the Montague situation."

"Did he ask you to go to the wedding with him?"

"No. Neither of us wanted the studio people to find out about us."

"Mrs Marshall has met you, I believe."

"That was an awkward time. I have never been introduced to the wife before. I definitely did not introduce William to my husband. Don't look so shocked, Chief Inspector. Women have affairs too, you know. At the moment adultery is not a crime, so what's the harm in a little bit extra sex and fun?"

"Mrs Marshall told me that you saw a photograph of Nicolette Du Bois and thought you had seen her somewhere before."

"Yes. I hardly slept for two nights trying to recall her."

"Have you ever done any modelling, especially glamour modelling?"

"Now, now, Chief Inspector. Just because I cheat on my husband does not make me the type of woman who drops them for the whole world to see."

"No, sorry, you misunderstand me. Nicolette Du Bois is a model who does bare everything for the camera."

"Oh, I see. The answer is no."

"Have you ever lived in France?"

"No, not lived there but Philip, my husband, and I visited Paris about ten years ago for a holiday. Hang on, that is it. Of course. How stupid of me. Philip and I were walking around one evening. To be honest, we were lost. We visited a lovely little park and were just walking up the road. There were very big houses on the right-hand side. We were on the other side. Suddenly a man came out of one of the houses. He was middle-aged and well dressed. He seemed a bit distressed. Anyway, he walked towards the park. About a minute later, a black-haired woman came running out of the same house. She was wearing a very short skirt and a bra, which seemed a bit odd as it was a chilly night. She ran towards the park and soon caught up with the man. She was shouting and seemed very angry. She grabbed his arm in quite an aggressive way and pulled him into the park. I asked Philip if we should go back to see if the man needed help, but he said we should get as far away as possible and let them sort it out. Obviously, that was some years ago and she is older now but that woman shouting and raving was Nicolette Du Bois. Definitely."

"Would your husband recognise her? I don't have to tell him where you saw the photograph if it would cause you problems."

"You can ask him, but I doubt if he would remember. For some reason, it stuck with me. I guess it is ridiculous to ask you if you know what happened."

"I do know. The man either committed suicide or was murdered in the park, I'm afraid."

Diana begins to weep. "Oh no. We should have gone back. Are you suggesting this Du Bois woman killed him?"

"I do not know but it is possible. I must ask you not to mention this to anyone just now, including your husband.

Do not feel bad about this. You had no way of knowing what would happen and you and Philip might have been attacked yourselves. I need you to make a formal statement about this. Is it alright if I send an officer round to your house when you are on your own?"

"Tomorrow night. I get home about six. Philip claims to be working late but that is when he sees his bit on the side. He will not be back until at least ten."

"Excellent. I will send someone round tomorrow night. Thank you for your help."

*

The following evening finds CI Melville working quietly in his office when Duty Sergeant Hollis rushes in. "Sir, we've received an emergency signal from PC Whittaker. She's not answering the radio. I've put out an urgent call for all officers anywhere near to drop what they are doing and go to help."

"Where is she?"

"Taking the statement from your Mrs Sheriff."

"Find three or four available officers and a specialist driver. Get a van ready to go. I will meet them outside in two minutes. Keep trying the radio."

Seven minutes later, the Chief Inspector and his team arrive at the house after a whirlwind journey that would normally take at least twenty minutes. There are several officers outside the house. The most senior, Sergeant Matthews, comes over immediately to Melville.

"Sir, PC Whittaker is conscious but she's bleeding heavily from the back of her head. She's dazed and very confused. An ambulance is on its way. The other lady is dead, one bullet to the brain."

"Her name is Diana Sheriff. Her husband will be home at ten. I know what he is doing but I have no idea where he is."

"We will try to find a phone number for him."

"Do not bother. I can guarantee he has turned his phone off."

CI Melville then enters the property. Mrs Sheriff is lying forwards over a dining table. There is a large pool of blood on the floor and a gun is lying in the middle of it. On the other side of the table lies PC June Whittaker being attended to by two male police officers. She is conscious and when she sees the Chief Inspector, she hesitantly whispers, "Sorry, sir."

"June, you have nothing to apologise for. If you hadn't lost consciousness, you would probably be dead as well. Can you remember anything?"

"We were writing out the statement," she stops and recovers her breath. "Suddenly there was someone else in the room. Small for a man. Dark clothing and a mask. Then I was hit and that's it."

"That is very helpful. Well done tonight."

At this point, two paramedics arrive and take over PC Whittaker's care. Melville locates Sergeant Matthews. "I brought four officers with me. I want two of them to go with her in the ambulance and guard her until I send replacements. Can you organise door-to-door enquiries? Do we know how the intruder got in?"

"Through the big windows at the back. They were fully open when we arrived. We found a half-completed statement form on the desk, covered in blood. It doesn't mention any specific names or locations."

"Pity. I spoke to Mrs Sheriff yesterday. So I know what she was going to say. What is worrying me is how they knew she was providing us with crucial information. I told her not to mention this to anyone. Could you stay here until the husband returns at ten o'clock? Ask him if he knew his wife was expecting a visit from the police tonight. I will come here tomorrow to talk to him properly. Is there anyone here who can drive me back to Westminster? I need to make some calls on the way."

In the back seat of a patrol car being driven at about half the speed of the outward journey, Melville rings Sergeant Adams who has returned to his position at Downing Street. "Is the House of Commons still sitting?"

"Yes, sir. They are voting on keeping or abandoning Trident, for about the fiftieth time."

"Good. I want you to find David McDougall and take him and his family to a safe house. He will object but tell him you have my full authority to put him in a cell if he doesn't cooperate. You can tell him what has happened tonight and that I am not in the mood to take any chances."

"I take it something has happened, sir."

"Marshall's girlfriend has been killed. There was a policewoman there taking a statement. She's been taken to hospital with head injuries but should pull through. The girlfriend is dead. It has been made to look like suicide, but we know, of course, that somebody else was there. So this one is a clear-cut murder. I believe McDougall is the next target, so find him urgently and let me know when they are safely tucked up with armed officers inside and out. Also can you upgrade to armed officers for Molan and Du Bois? They should be back in their apartment by now."

The next call is to Claude Abbeye. "We've got another one tonight. Marshall's girlfriend. This time, though, there was a police officer there taking a statement from her, so we know this one is murder. I thought we had finally made a breakthrough. The woman saw Du Bois chase a man into a park in Paris ten years ago. She recognised her from the wedding invitation Nic and Sara sent to Marshall. All I can do is formally record what she told me yesterday and put it with the partly finished statement. If we can get the bloodstains off it, of course."

"Is your officer alright?"

"She has got a serious head wound but she is conscious now, so she should make a full recovery in time. I will get a full statement from her tomorrow, but she told me earlier that her attacker was short for a man and wore a mask covering their face. We certainly are not going to get an identification from her."

"They are getting desperate now. This is the nearest

they have come to a mistake. Your pressure must be getting to them."

"I need to check with the officer at their house what time they went in and out today. I will tear my hair out if they have both been in all day."

"I will get Paris to talk again to neighbours and I will go through the files again. I take it your witness did not see what happened in the park."

"She wanted to, but her husband dragged her away. I'll keep in touch."

By this time, the car is turning into the police station car park. Melville thanks the driver and enters the station. He is met immediately by Sergeant Hollis.

"How is she?"

"She is in hospital She has a bad head injury, but she should be fine. I've got officers inside and outside her room."

"I've located her mother. She lives in Newcastle, so I'll ring her and tell her the situation is under control and she doesn't need to rush down here."

"When did PC Whittaker know she was going to the Sheriff's house?"

"About half an hour before she left. She was supposed to be working with PC Bernard from traffic, but they had enough of their own officers, so she was stood down."

"I want to check her personal mobile."

"It will be in her locker. I've got the master key."

The phone is on top of her civilian clothes. Melville

checks it and says, "She made one call this morning and nothing since."

Sergeant Hollis takes the phone and comments, "That is her mother's number. She had no idea she was going there when she made that call."

"That is good news. Somebody leaked the fact a police officer was taking a statement. The killer wanted to prevent her putting her story in writing."

"As far as I know, PC Whittaker and myself were the only ones who knew where she was going. I promise you I would never put any officer at risk by blabbing. I blame myself for this. I should have sent two officers."

"It is not your fault and I know you would never talk out of turn. Can you ask the entire shift if she told anybody what she was doing?"

"Yes, sir."

Melville's mobile rings before he can get to his office.

"Sir, it's Sergeant Adams. Mr McDougall is insisting on talking to you."

"Hello, Mr McDougall. How can I help you?"

"This is preposterous. I refuse to have my life and my family's lives disrupted because you are panicking."

"I am sure Sergeant Adams has explained the position to you. I have lost an important witness and nearly lost a brilliant officer tonight. Friends and acquaintances of Sara Molan and Nicolette Du Bois are being eliminated one by one. If you are not already top of the list, you must be extremely close. I do not intend to allow anyone a free shot at you or anyone else I consider to be in danger. Now I will give you a choice. Cooperate with the Sergeant and help him get you and your family safely settled as soon as possible or I will have you arrested for wilful obstruction of a police investigation. When you appear in court, I will vehemently oppose bail. At least I will know where you are once you are in prison. Your choice."

"Alright. You win, but I still think this is unnecessary."

"Good. Now could you pass me back to Sergeant Adams, please?"

"Hello. He has agreed now. If he messes you about or tries to change his mind, arrest him immediately on suspicion of wilful obstruction. Do not let him have any wriggling room at all."

"Yes, sir."

*

Two hours later, it is Sergeant Matthews' turn to call the Chief Inspector. "Sir, I've got Mr Sheriff with me. He had no idea his wife was expecting the police tonight. He says she spends Tuesday evenings with her boyfriend, although he doesn't know who he is."

"Interesting. Can I speak to him? Mr Sheriff, I am Chief Inspector Melville. Please accept my condolences on your loss. I know it is a difficult time for you, but I would like to ask you a few questions please. Where have you been tonight?"

"At work."

"Your wife thought you saw your girlfriend every Tuesday."

"I do not have a girlfriend. Diana has always been the only girl I want."

"Has your wife been upset recently?"

"Yes, but she refused to tell me why."

"Her boyfriend, who it appears she met every Tuesday, died a few days ago. His name was William Marshall and they both worked at the TV studio."

"Is that why you wanted a statement?"

"No. She was giving us a statement about something that occurred when you were in Paris ten years ago. Do you remember anything unusual happening?"

"It was a lovely break. That is all I remember."

"Do you remember a woman chasing after a man just after you left a park, while you were walking around Paris?"

"Good grief. Was Diana still worrying about that? I do vaguely remember that she wanted to go and interfere, but I flatly refused. There are enough crazy people over here but in a foreign country tourists need to keep well away from any kind of trouble."

"Do you remember anything about the woman?"

"She was virtually naked. I remember that. She had the shortest skirt I have ever seen and just a bra on the top half."

"What about her hair or her face?"

"No idea. I did not see her face. Are you saying my wife died because of something that happened a decade ago in another country?"

"Your wife saw a photograph of someone she felt she had seen before. I saw her yesterday and she realised that it was the woman she saw chasing a middle-aged gentleman towards the park in Paris. I told her not to tell anyone about it and we would take her statement tonight. Nothing is certain but I am afraid there is a good chance somebody decided to ensure she could not put her story in writing. Is there anyone you can think of who she might have told that the police were coming to see her?"

"Oh God. I'm going to have to tell her mother. I just don't think I can do it. She wouldn't have told anyone else."

"If you give her details to the Sergeant, he will contact her for you. Is there anything you want to ask me?"

"No."

"I will need to talk to you again, but it can wait until you are over the initial shock. I am going to leave officers outside your property tonight. If you would rather go to a hotel to avoid the mess downstairs, then Sergeant Matthews can arrange that at our expense."

*

The next morning, CI Melville checks on the current situation. The McDougall family are under armed guard in a police safe house. Philip Sheriff is in a hotel. Diana Sheriff's mother was visited last night by two family liaison officers who broke the news of her daughter's death as gently as possible. PC June Whittaker remains in hospital drifting in and out of consciousness and is due to undergo scans later today. Information has come in from the officer posted outside Sara and Nic's property that they went out in their car at three PM to go shopping and returned just after eight PM with several bags from an upmarket London emporia.

The Chief Inspector decides he has three priorities that day. To find out who knew about Diana Sheriff giving a statement, to speak to Sara and Nic and finally to interview June Whittaker as soon as she is well enough.

He soon has a visitor in Sergeant Hollis. The Sergeant says, "The tech boys have been over Mrs Sheriff's mobile. She made a call to a landline yesterday morning and had a call back from the same number. That is the number Mr Sheriff gave to Sergeant Matthews last night for us to contact his mother-in-law. The electoral roll shows a Mrs Kathleen Summers aged seventy. I've got the address, but there is a problem. Someone else is also listed at the address. A certain Ian Joseph Payne. He has over thirty convictions, mainly for theft but also for assault and GBH. I know him. He is trouble."

"Right. Bring them both in. Send two cars. I don't want them hatching up a story on the way in. Put them in separate interview rooms and let me know when they arrive."

Melville rings Sergeant Adams at home. "Do you fancy helping me interview Diana Sheriff's mother and her criminal partner?"

"I was on duty last night and again tonight. I need sleep."

"You're young. You will get over it. I am borrowing you again for a few days, so you can sleep soundly tonight."

"Do I have a choice?"

"No. We are picking them up in Romford right now. So, quick as you can."

"I wish you would find another Sergeant. You have had a vacancy for months."

"Why don't you come back permanently?"

"Frankly, I might just as well. I would only have one job to worry about then."

"Excellent, now get a move on."

*

Half an hour later, Mrs Summers and Mr Payne are ensconced in separate interview rooms and Sergeant Adams finally arrives.

CI Melville says, "We will start with Diana's mother, Mrs Summers. I want to know if her daughter told her about helping us and if so, who she told."

In the interview room, Sergeant Adams asks the questions after his boss offers condolences.

"Mrs Summers, did you speak to your daughter yesterday?"

"She rang me in the morning before she went to work. She sounded upset but wouldn't say why. I rang her back later at work and invited her over last night. That useless husband of hers visits his girlfriend every Tuesday, so sometimes she comes over to us. She said no. The police were coming round to take a statement or something."

"Did she say exactly why the police were coming?"

"It was something to do with seeing someone she recognised from Paris when she was there years ago. Beats me what she was on about."

"Did she say a name for this person she recognised?"

"No."

"Did you tell anyone about the police visit?"

"No." Kathleen Summers pauses. "We have several phones around the house and Ian often listens in to my conversations on one of the extensions."

"Do you think he listened in when you spoke to your daughter?"

"I think he did. He usually does."

"Thank you, Mrs Summers. We'll get an officer to take your statement."

Outside, the two policemen confer.

"Do you believe her?" asks Sergeant Adams.

"Yes, I do. I think she is too shocked by her daughter's murder to lie. Let's move on to Payne. My turn," responds the Chief Inspector.

Ian Payne is heavily tattooed, tall, well-built and in a bad mood.

"Where the hell have you been? I've been here for hours," is his opening gambit.

"We have been talking to Kathleen Summers and, as she has just lost her daughter, we took things slowly," replies Melville with great restraint.

"Yeah. Well, get on with it now you're here."

"Did you listen in to your partner's phone calls with her daughter yesterday?"

"Naw, I wouldn't do that."

"According to Mrs Summers, you do it all the time," Melville says sternly. "Now stop pissing me about. I have an officer in hospital and I have your stepdaughter's murder to solve. Added to which I am in a foul mood, so you had better start talking before I lose my temper. Right, now we will start again. Did you listen in to those phone calls?"

"Yeah. Kath asked her stuck-up daughter to come over that evening. I thought that was our chance."

"Your chance to do what?"

"Rob her house. That useless husband of hers is off shagging his bit of stuff every Tuesday. So I rang a mate of mine and told him it was all clear. Then that bitch said she wasn't coming so I had to cancel it."

"What is your mate's name?"

"Naw. I never divulge my sources. Data Protection Act."

"Mr Payne, you are not running a multinational consortium. You are a nasty petty criminal who is prepared to rob his partner's daughter to make a few quid. Now what is his name?"

"John Turney. We've worked together for years. I was going to stay home and make sure Diana stayed for a couple of hours. John was going to grab what he could.

She had some lovely jewellery. Don't suppose you know if she's left it to Kath?"

"I will get someone to take your statement. Then you can both go."

Melville and Adams go to see Sergeant Hollis. The Chief Inspector states, "Get someone to take his statement and then send them both home. Ever heard of a John Turney?"

"It's like oldies day in here today. John Turney. Known associates, Ian Payne. Got a string of convictions. Most recent last October. Six months on one burglary charge with five others considered. He was out in three."

"Can you find him?"

"I've got an address he went to three months ago. We will start there and maybe we'll get lucky. He lives with a prostitute. Oh. What's her name? Unusual first name. Scarlet. Scarlet Mahoney. Nasty piece of work. Tried to cut off one client's pride and joy with a penknife."

They leave Hollis to his reminiscences and retreat to Melville's office. Barely two minutes later, Sergeant Hollis rushes in without knocking. "Sir, you need to get over to Molan's place urgent. There's been an incident. One person believed to be dead."

*

When they arrive at the scene, the two police guarding the newlyweds are standing together, a few metres away from a prone figure on the pavement. The victim is wearing identical clothes to PC Whittaker's attacker including a mask that has been removed and placed by the body. A gun lies nearby. The person shot is a young woman, possibly in her early to mid-twenties, with short blonde hair. The two armed guards are standing over by the entrance to the house. Chief Inspector Melville goes over to them and introduces himself. One of the officers still has his gun, so Melville addresses his questions to the other man, "Are you alright?"

"A bit shaken. My first fatal."

"Could you talk me through what happened?"

"The victim arrived in the white car and parked down the road. She attracted my attention because she was messing about doing something. I think now it was the face mask she was putting on. She could not drive here with it on. She got out of the car and started to walk towards me. There was something in her left hand. As she got closer, I could see it was a gun. I shouted to her to drop the gun, but she just kept walking slowly forwards. It was almost as if she was in a trance. She just kept coming towards me with her eyes fixed firmly on me. I shouted again that she must put down the gun or I would shoot to kill. She stopped where she fell. She slowly raised the gun and pointed it straight at me. I used my radio to yell to my colleague to get the residents safe. She was still pointing the gun at me, so I told her I would shoot if she didn't lower the gun. I honestly thought she had gone for the trigger, so I shot her and she went down. I rushed over to her, but it was obvious there was no point in doing first aid."

"You did what you were trained to do. You may have saved three other lives today. If what you have told me is true then you have nothing to fear from the investigation. If you do, contact me and I will support you. Now, where is your gun?"

"I gave it to the most senior officer from the first wave of assistance. That is the correct procedure. He will keep it until the Shooting Investigation Unit arrive."

Turning to the other officer, Melville asks, "What happened from your point of view?"

"I was inside and the residents were in the main room downstairs. On my radio, I got a shouted warning to get the ladies safe. I bundled them into the downstairs office because that has a key. I told them to lie on the floor and then I locked them in. I ran outside just in time to see and hear the shooting. I also ran to the victim to try and help her but she was dead before she hit the ground. My opinion is we did everything by the book. We did our job. The baddie is dead and the goodies all survived."

"It is never that simple. We all have good and bad in us to some degree, but I do agree you did everything right. How are Nic and Sara?"

"They are deeply shocked. There is an ambulance on the way but I don't think they need to go to hospital. They are back in the main room and they have broken out the brandy."

"Could you tell them I will visit them later, but just at the moment I need to be in about three places at once."

He then joins Sergeant Adams, "Anything?"

"The gun hasn't been fired. There is one bullet in it. There is no identification on her. The Medical Examiner turned her over and she has some very faint scars on her back. Looks as if she has been severely flogged at some point."

"Get her fingerprints and run them through the system. If she fell foul of Godwin and his whippings, she should be on file."

"Yes, sir."

"Stay here now. Liaise with Sergeant Hollis if anything important crops up. I want that identification asap."

*

Back at the station, Chief Inspector Melville uses Sergeant Hollis as a sounding board for his thoughts.

"There was only one bullet in the gun. Why was she picking a fight with the guard outside? If she shot him, she would be out of bullets. She did not shoot him and now she is dead."

"Suicide by copper. It does happen."

"I would agree if she had been dressed in any way other than identically to whoever murdered Diana Sheriff last night."

"Perhaps she did kill her and did not want to spend her life in prison. Maybe she was after the armed officer?"

"His own wife could not identify him once he is

all dressed up like an alien skywalker. She might have wanted to take out a policeman, but if that was the case, why did she not even take a shot?"

"This is a crazy case, sir. It feels as if we are attempting to put together a huge jigsaw puzzle with some pieces missing and some pieces that belong to a different puzzle altogether."

"What is the connection between this woman and Molan and Du Bois?"

"If they were the target then there must be a reason. You don't just turn up outside someone's house and start shooting at complete strangers. Unless you are a terrorist, of course."

"Well, she did not shout, 'God is great' or White lives matter too'. So I doubt if this is terror related. We are missing something but heaven only knows what it is."

Sergeant Hollis leaves but is back in five minutes. "We've identified the victim. Name is Linda Taylor, age twenty one. Three convictions as an adult, two for prostitution and one for possession of a controlled substance. Heroin in this case. She did three months of a six-month sentence and was released just before last Christmas."

"Address?"

"Only when she was arrested last year."

"Send someone out there and make enquiries whether she is still there or moved on."

"Yes, sir. There is something else. Linda Taylor has a juvenile conviction when she was thirteen-years-old. She had a fight at school with another thirteen year old girl.

Taylor half killed her, broke her cheekbone, blacked both her eyes, ripped out chunks of her hair and then smashed her head down into the playground surface a couple of times. Taylor got six months in a youth detention centre and one hundred and fifty strokes of the cat."

"Sergeant Adams said she had faint whip marks on her back. Can you do a bit of digging into this? What was the fight about? Who was the other girl? What happened to her?"

"Yes, sir."

Half an hour later, Sergeant Hollis is back again, "The other girl is Shirley Pomfrey. Linda Taylor was trying to steal her boyfriend. They agreed that whoever won would claim him. Taylor won and Pomfrey went to hospital. She was charged with having sex whilst unmarried and underage. She got two and a half years in youth detention, a lot of caning and flogging and she was branded as a slut. I have tracked her down and spoken to her. She seems a very unhappy person. She certainly won't shed any tears over Taylor's death."

"Can you give Sergeant Adams the details and get him to go and see her? I want to know who the boyfriend was and whether Ms Pomfrey is willing to testify if we can track him down. I'm going to the hospital."

*

PC June Whittaker is lying in bed in a ward that has been cleared of other patients. There is an armed officer outside the ward and another inside. Her mother is sitting by her daughter's bedside. Melville introduces himself and then asks June, "How are you?"

"I am aching but it is getting better slowly. I have concussion but nothing is broken, which is a relief. If it is alright with you, sir, I would like to go back to Newcastle when I am fit enough to leave hospital."

"I think that is a great idea. Take as much time as you need to fully recover."

"Do I have to have armed officers here round the clock?"

"Well, you won't need them in Newcastle. I suppose nobody has told you. A young woman pulled a gun on an armed officer protecting Sara Molan today. That is why I have not been able to come earlier. Whilst there is any threat at all, I'm afraid I cannot relax the protection."

"Was anyone hurt?"

"The young woman was killed." Mrs Whittaker looks shocked at this. Melville continues, "Today's attacker is around five feet two inches. Do you think that fits the person who hit you?"

"No. He or she is taller than that. Five six at least, possibly five eight."

"Alright. I will leave you in your mother's care. Thank you for your bravery yesterday. If you had not pressed the emergency button, it could have been hours before anyone found you. Look after yourself. Do exactly what the doctors and your mother tell you and you will be fine."

*

Sergeant Hollis is waiting to pounce when the Chief Inspector returns.

"Sergeant Adams has phoned in. He says Shirley Pomfrey is too terrified to go out, even now when she can cover up her branding. Her back is badly scarred, like Taylor's but much worse. She is willing to testify, but how good a witness she will be is difficult to gauge. She has revealed the boyfriend's name. At the time, apparently, he threatened to set his father on them and their families if Taylor or Ms Pomfrey revealed his name. I've written the name on a piece of paper, because I reckon the fewer people around here who know who it is, the better."

Melville takes the paper and looks at the details written on it. "Right. Time to get the Turneys in. I want the whole family in. You can bring in the dog and cat if they have one. I will probably get more sense out of them than I will from the humans. If Sergeant Adams isn't back in time, I will need you to sit in with me for the interviews."

Sergeant Adams arrives back before the Turneys are brought in. Melville takes the opportunity to catch up.

"Shirley Pomfrey is a mess, sir," begins Adams. "She and Taylor paid a terrible price, whilst the boyfriend walked away free."

"Has she seen Taylor since?"

"No. Pomfrey came out of youth detention just before her sixteenth birthday, so she never went back to school. She hasn't seen the boyfriend since either. How is June Whittaker?"

"Not too bad, considering what she has been through. She is going to take a break with her mother. I have chickened out of telling Sergeant Hollis yet. It has been a bad enough day without upsetting him."

The Turneys arrive ten minutes later, without any pets.

"Where do you want to start?" Sergeant Adams asks.

"Let's go for the son, Luke," comes the reply.

"This should be fun."

"You can lead on him. You will be spending all day long doing this when you make Inspector."

Luke Turney is lounging back in his chair with his feet on the table when the two policemen enter the interview room. One inspectorial look from Adams is enough to make him sit properly.

"What the fuck is going on here? I ain't done nothin'," snorts Luke.

"Stop swearing. I am not going to swear at you." retorts Sergeant Adams. "A woman called Linda Taylor was killed today. Do you know her?"

"Never heard of her."

"Now, that is strange, because you spent three years in the same class. When you were thirteen, you were having sex with Shirley Pomfrey when Linda decided she wanted you. They had a huge fight and Shirley ended up in hospital. Then they both ended up in youth detention. Do you remember yet?"

"Why waste your time asking me if you already know the fucking answer?"

"This is your final warning. Do not swear. Do you admit that you knew Linda Taylor at school?"

"Yeah."

"And was Shirley Pomfrey your girlfriend when you were both thirteen?"

"Yeah, for a while. There have been so many that I forget when and where, you know."

"Were any of the others underage?"

"No comment."

"You know, I think I liked you better when you were lying."

"I ain't lying."

"I tell you what. We will start all over again and this time I want the truth. You are already facing a charge of underage sex. I would strongly advise you not to add wilful obstruction as well. Do you know Linda Taylor?"

"Yeah. I never had her though. She won the fight but was sent to youth prison or something. When she came back to school she went into a different class and she kept out of my way. I think of her every day and how she got away. I'd give anything to shag her just once."

"When did you last see her?"

"At school." Suddenly, Luke slumps in his chair and looks close to tears. "Look. If I tell you the truth, can you put in a good word over the sex? It was years ago."

Melville nods and Adams speaks, "Yes, we'll do what we can. Now, what do you want to tell us?"

"The only girl I have ever really wanted is Linda. She was so beautiful, even at thirteen. Great figure, a wonderful laugh and a reputation for being an ice queen. And she fought to get me. Then she was gone but I always thought I would get her one day. About two months ago, Dad went out on the booze one night. When he came home, pissed out of his skull, he grabbed me and said, 'I had a tom tonight. She was wonderful. The best I have ever had and do you know who she is? Linda Taylor. The girl of your dreams. I have had her, son, and I am going to have her again. There isn't a damn thing you can do about it. Loser.' It broke my heart. I have nightmares about it to this day."

"Do you know when he last saw her?"

"I think he saw her once more. He said she wanted more money than they agreed, cos she needed drugs. I think he was afraid of catching something off her."

"Where did he meet her?"

"King's Cross, I expect. That's where he usually goes when Scarlet won't open her legs for him."

"Where was your father last night?"

"Home, all night."

"Luke, we have said we will help you. We do not have to, so let's try again. Where was your father last night?"

"He went out about six and came back about half seven with some stuff."

"Stuff he stole?"

"I don't ask any more."

Melville intervenes now, "Sergeant, could you hand

Luke over to the Custody Officer? We will keep you here tonight and put you in front of a magistrate tomorrow. We will not oppose bail so you should be back with your loving family before dark."

*

Sergeant Adams returns a few minutes later.

"Well done," says CI Melville. "I think you can manage without any tips from me."

"That was an easy one. I could tell when he was lying. His lips moved and words came out. Who's next?"

"The delicate Scarlet. I will question her and then we can both try to get some sense out of father."

Scarlet Mahoney looks about fifty years old but is probably ten to fifteen years younger than that. For some reason, she is wearing a sleeveless top, which reveals lines and marks from needles on both arms. She is also wearing a very short skirt, which reveals that she is wearing stockings and suspenders rather than tights. This may attract people at King's Cross but it makes the two police officers feel nauseous.

"Why am I here? I ain't done nothin'," she exclaims as soon as they walk in.

"You are here to answer some questions. We have just been messed about by Luke, so all I need from you is the truth. If you lie, I am quite happy to arrest you for wilful obstruction in a police investigation. Let us start with an easy one. Where was John Turney last evening?"

"Indoors with me all evening and night."

"Right, that is your first lie. You have two more lives and then you win a night in our cells. Luke is already there, so it will feel just like home sweet home. Where was John Turney?"

"He was with me from about half seven or quarter to eight. He went out just before six."

"Where did he go?"

"How the hell would I know? Probably with some slag, though it usually takes him about two minutes not an hour and a half."

"Did he bring any stuff home with him?"

"What, drugs? No, we are not into that."

"That is lie number two. If you wanted me to believe that you should have covered your arms. They are covered in tracks and marks and most of them look recent to me. I am not really interested in drugs today. Did he bring home any stolen goods?"

"Dunno. I don't want to know."

"Do you know a woman called Linda Taylor?"

Scarlet laughs vigorously. "She's no woman. She's just a common slut. I have never met her, but in between John telling me every night I am not as good as she is and Luke mooning around dreaming of fucking her, I hate every inch of her. I hope she's in trouble."

"She was killed earlier today. I suppose that counts as trouble. What do you know about her?"

"She went to school with Luke. She fancied him. Stupid cow. Instead of just dragging him behind the bike sheds and shagging him, she decides to beat the crap out of his girlfriend. They both ended up in youth detention or summat. Never saw either of them again. She was blonde then, pretty little thing in those days."

"Are you still on the game?"

"Only when John gambles away his money before he even gets home."

"Ever work King's Cross nowadays?"

"No. John goes there when I am mad with him. If I work at all, it is usually round Soho somewhere. Bigger area and less of you lot. I'll give you both a discount if you are interested."

Melville changes the subject quickly.

"Ever heard of Ian Payne?"

"Now I can help you with him. Payne by name and pain in the arse by nature. He used to do houses and stuff with John. He's a total waste of space. John has nothing to do with him now."

"Is that another lie or is that what he told you?"

"That is what he told me. If he is hanging round with that loser, I will cut his balls off."

"Payne told us he spoke to John yesterday to arrange a job. He later cancelled it but I think John went ahead with it anyway. Do you know a Diana Sheriff?"

"Is that the one who got shot last night?"

"Yes."

"Well, I heard about it on the telly but I'd never heard of her before. Hang on, are you saying John was going to rob her house last night, found her in and topped her? He is a lot of things – a thief, a lousy lover and a shocking provider, but he's not a killer. No way. You can tell him from me that if he is dealing with Ian Payne again he had better find somewhere else to sleep tonight or he will regret it."

"Right, no more questions. I will get an officer to take your statement about Linda Taylor and when your husband was out last night. If I find out you have told me any other lies, then you will be going into a cell. Otherwise, you can go home when I have finished with John."

"What do you think?" Chief Inspector Melville asks when they are outside.

"I think if I lived with her, I would cut my own balls off. What an awful woman."

"Yes. Somebody loves her though, just like Emily."

"Sorry, sir. I don't understand that. Who's Emily?"

"Bagpuss. He was only a saggy cloth cat but Emily loved him, or something like that." Sergeant Adams still looks confused. "Oh, please do not tell me you have never watched Bagpuss. For heaven's sake, what is this world coming to?"

"Before my time, sir."

Melville looks sullen but makes no response. He thinks for a few seconds then speaks, "Come on, we'll see John Turney now."

*

John Turney is in his fifties, covered in tattoos and very big. Definitely not the right person to be tackling at ten o'clock at night when sleep-deprived. CI Melville introduces himself and Sergeant Adams. "We are both tired so we will ask you some questions and you answer them truthfully and we can all go home. Do you know Ian Payne?"

"Never heard of him."

"Then let me remind you. You have three joint convictions for burglary and he phoned you at least twice yesterday. So, have another go."

"Yeah, I know him. We used to do the odd job together."

"Why did he ring you? Before you answer, perhaps you should consider that I already know the answer."

"He offered me a job for that night. His wife's daughter was coming over to them. He told me she was going there straight from work and her husband would be out until ten. He said they were rich and he gave me the address. Then he rings back and says she is not coming. She has got the cops coming to take a statement about something that happened in Paris years ago."

"So did you have a nice quiet night in with Scarlet?"

"You don't have quiet nights in with Scarlet. That bitch always wants something. Nag, nag, nag. I thought I would see if Payne was having me on and doing the job himself. When I get there I see a police car outside, so I went further down the street and found an empty place. So I did that one instead. When I came out, it was like a scene out of The Sweeney. Cops everywhere. I got out of there quick."

"Did you steal anything?"

"Not much. The place was virtually empty but I got a few scraps."

"Give it back and I will forget about it."

"Fine."

Sergeant Adams takes over the questioning at this point, "Payne told you the police were coming round, and you saw that for yourself. Did you tell anyone about that?"

"I told Big Al."

"Who's Big Al?"

"A guy I do business with sometimes. I sell him stuff."

"Stolen goods."

"No. He sells on information. Things I hear or find out about. Just things I discover out and about."

"Or in people's houses."

"No comment."

"What is Big Al's surname?"

"No idea. All contact is by phone. I have the number but he won't answer a strange number. I have never met him. I phone him the information and if he gets anything for it, he gives me half."

"Why on earth would Big Al be interested in the police visiting Diana Sheriff?"

"A few weeks ago, Al rang me. He sometimes does some driving and he works for the TV studios. He had dropped a lady at the studio and she asked him to let her know if he got any info on someone."

"Diana Sheriff?"

"No. William Marshall."

"Did he tell you who asked him?"

"Not by name but he was taking this woman from Marshall's house to the studio so she could go with him to some function that night."

"So, what happened next?"

"Al rang me, asked me to snoop about a bit and find some dirt. I watched Marshall's house for days and then he goes out in his car about nine one night and I followed him. He went to the studio and made a call. Sure enough, some woman comes out and gets in the car with him. They drive to a cheap hotel and go in. I thought I would be there all night but about forty-five minutes later they come out. He gets in the car and drives off. Then a taxi comes for her, so I follow it and get the address. The next day I go over there, slip the postie a tenner and get her name. Diana Sheriff. Then I tells Al and he puts fifty quid through my letterbox the next day. Forty quid profit. Anyway, Marshall gets snuffed, but Big Al says watch the girlfriend. The woman is still interested in her. So when Payne rings me, I think if I'm in her house I will do a thorough job on it and find out all I can about this woman. When he cancelled it, I rang Big Al with what I'd got, which was really just the police coming. He rang back later. Said the woman was delighted but didn't need any more stuff now. Mind you, he says there's fifty coming my way. That's it. I have nothing else to give you."

Melville takes over now, "I need a statement. When we have that, I will release you and Scarlet with no charges. Officers will take you home and recover everything you took last night. If you mess them about they will take your house apart looking for anything that doesn't belong."

Outside, they retreat to Melville's office. The CI speaks first, "I need to talk through this. Elizabeth Marshall asks her driver to dig the dirt on her husband and he comes up with Diana Sheriff. But she already knows about her. They have even met."

"She probably did not have an address."

"That's probably right. Then Marshall is killed."

"By her?"

"No. I'm thinking about Hollis' jigsaw puzzle with pieces that don't belong. Marshall fits the whole suicide or murder theme. If she killed him, she would have made it look like murder, not suicide, because of the insurance policy. So, Elizabeth is in a pickle. No husband, no payout and a grieving mistress. So, she comes to see me and tells this true story about Diana Sheriff recognising Du Bois. That helps to link the subsequent events to the previous killings. When she gets the information from Big Al, she draws up a plan. She will break in to Sheriff's house when the police are there, take out the officer, kill Diana and make it look like suicide. She knew some police presence was there because June Whittaker left the car outside. That scared off Turney but not Mrs Marshall."

"But why, sir?"

"Money. Marshall's death will be ruled suicide. By killing his girlfriend in the same way, but ensuring it would be treated as a murder because PC Whittaker was attacked by a third party at the scene, she hoped it would be deemed murder at the inquest. Then she would come to us saying if Sheriff was murdered, so was my husband."

"Good theory. Where is the proof?"

"Turney and Big Al."

"Wonderful witnesses, sir. Any half-decent defence lawyer will rip them to pieces."

"I think we don't need anything but their words. We will go and see Molan and Du Bois. In the meantime, get officers round to Mrs Marshall and arrest her on suspicion of the murder of Diana Sheriff and assault on June Whittaker. She should be waiting for us when we get back."

"What about some sleep, sir?"

"You can sleep all day tomorrow. Come on."

*

The armed officer outside the Molan residence eyes them suspiciously as Melville parks the car.

"Get your ID out," he says to Adams. "I do not want another shooting today."

They approach the officer warily. He looks at the ID cards and waves them through. There is another armed officer inside. He stops them and speaks, "Can I talk to you? There's something wrong with today's shooting."

"Go on," responds Melville.

"The woman gets out of her car and walks towards the officer with a gun in her left hand. They are saying it was suicide by cop. But how did she know he was armed? His gun was in the holster. You would need very good sight to see the gun from where she parked."

"She could have seen the gun earlier. All she had to do was drive past slowly."

"We are professionals. I have worked with this officer for ten years. He can spot a car going past more than once in an instant. If she had driven past on his shift, he would have remembered."

"So, what are you saying?"

"It is a set-up. He said she seemed to be in a trance. I reckon somebody drugged her and sent her to wave a pistol at an armed officer."

"Murder by cop rather than suicide?"

"Yes, sir."

"I need to think about this. But thank you. How are the ladies?"

"Terrified. On their fourth bottle of brandy. You won't get much sense out of them."

"I never do," says Melville sadly.

They move into the main living room. Sara and Nic are cuddled together on the settee, drinking brandy.

"How are you both?" the Chief Inspector asks.

"Still shocked," Molan replies. "I don't think the brandy is doing anything for the shock but it's certainly working for our libido."

"What do you remember about the incident?"

"We were sitting in here and one of the guards comes dashing in, grabs me by the arm and yanks me next door into the office. Nic is following and he shoves her in. He tells us to lie flat under a desk or table and then he locks us in. At first, a man was shouting occasionally. Then there was a shot about thirty seconds later and everybody seemed to be running around and shouting. It seemed like ages before we were let out. Were they after us?"

"At present I would say no. I do not think it is connected to the previous suicides. It is different. Possibly, a copycat. Do you know Diana Sheriff?"

"Of course I do. She works next to me. Why?"

"She was killed last night. She was Marshall's latest girlfriend. Did you know that?"

"Not a clue. Mind you, she is classier than most of his conquests. Was she shot?"

"Yes and one of my officers was badly hurt. She was there when the attacker struck so we know it was murder this time. Another copycat killing."

Nic looks confused, "I don't understand. You are saying there is more than one person going around making murders into suicides."

"Yes. I think the person who shot Godwin has

probably done at least five other similar killings in France, and Montague and Marshall over here. But someone else killed Diana Sheriff and I hope to make an arrest when I leave here. Linda Taylor was the girl shot out here. She was, I believe, drugged and sent by another person to her death. Did either of you know Linda? Twenty-one years old, short blonde hair and a convicted prostitute."

Both women shake their heads.

Melville continues, "Do you want to stay here? Or would you prefer to go elsewhere for a few days. I can offer a safe house or another safe house where you would be sharing with the McDougall family or a hotel?"

"Are you going to keep our guards if we stay here?" asks Nic.

"Yes, for the time being."

"Then we stay here. We know now they can protect us and keep us safe. It was horrible but they did their job wonderfully. We owe them our lives."

"I am sure they will be awarded medals of some kind. They acted brilliantly. I know you were pushed about but it was necessary."

"We would like to thank them, personally."

There is something about the way Nic lingers on the final word that suggests the thank you might go further than a handshake and a peck on the cheek.

Outside, Melville says to Sergeant Adams and the officer, "I want to carry out an experiment. I am going to walk down to where the car was parked and come towards you slowly. I shall be holding something in my left hand and I want one of you to shout when you can clearly see what is in my hand. I will shout when I can see the officer's gun."

"Is he always like this?" the officer asks Adams.

"Only when there is a full moon. I mean there are street lights but it is night-time, not the middle of the day."

A distant voice interrupts, "Right, shout when you see what I am holding." Melville advances slowly, his left arm held horizontally in front of him.

As he approaches the shooting site, Adams finally yells, "You've got your mobile phone. I can just see it now."

Melville replies, "I still can't make out the gun and this is where Linda Taylor got shot." He then continues to advance, eventually saying that he can now see the gun properly.

When the Chief Inspector rejoins the others, the guard asks, "What on earth was that all about?"

"It was about proving that she could not have known the officer was armed when she was shot. She was out of her skull on something. She was doing what she was told to do. Keep walking towards the officer pointing your gun at him. We will probably never know why she agreed to it. This was a cold-blooded murder using a police shooter as the murder weapon."

"Alright, sir," says Sergeant Adams. "But who would stage something like this?"

"Someone who wanted us to connect it to the suicides because of the clothes worn and doing this outside Molan's property. This is another set of pieces that just do not fit in with the first two murders here and Godwin's in France. I know who did it and when we get back to the station, I will get them picked up. We can deal with them after we have got a confession from Mrs Marshall."

Adams groans and gets in the car. "Are you going to tell me who you are going to arrest, sir?"

"Of course. Shirley Pomfrey."

"Sir, with respect, that is crazy. She can barely leave the house. She is sectionable."

"That is what she told you. I am sure that I am right and if I am, I think Ms Pomfrey will be willing to admit to this. Her aim was to kill Linda Taylor without drawing any attention to herself. I imagine it was a shock to her to have Sergeant Hollis on the phone so soon after the incident. So she panicked and put on this "my life is ruined" act. I have done some checking, you know. She has a car registered to her and is a member of a local rambling group."

"I don't buy it, sir. I saw her. If that was an act then she should turn professional."

"Perhaps she will when she gets out of jail."

*

Back in the station, Melville gives a harassed Night Duty Sergeant instructions to send officers to arrest Shirley

Pomfrey. He is then informed that Elizabeth Marshall is in interview room three.

"I am not happy about going into an interview with just a theory and no evidence, sir," says a worried Sergeant Adams.

"We have evidence from Turney and Big Al. Don't worry. It will be fine. Come and learn."

They enter the interview room. Mrs Marshall is sitting at the table in the middle of the room. She looks calm and untroubled. The policemen sit on the other side of the table.

"Do you want a solicitor?" CI Melville asks.

"I have already been asked that and said no," Elizabeth replies. "Do I need one?"

"Well, that is up to you. If you do then we will have to delay this interview until tomorrow. The choice is yours."

"Come on, get on with it."

"What I am going to do is tell you how I think everything happened. If you disagree, please let me know. Once you got over the shock of losing your husband, you turned to more practical matters like money. It all seemed fine at first. Your husband had been murdered and you would inherit everything including the insurance monies. Then you realised that the inquest verdict would probably be suicide as has been the case in the vast majority of what I suppose we could call the suicide murders. I believe they are murders but I have no proof. They look like suicides and that is the usual verdict. That, of course, would leave you penniless. So you came to see me. You told me the true story of how Diana Sheriff recognised Nicolette Du Bois. I went to see her and the next night I arranged for an officer to visit her to take a statement. You knew about the second meeting because Big Al told you. It was obviously of interest to you because you paid him one hundred pounds for that information."

"Two hundred," Elizabeth says resignedly.

"I stand corrected. So, you decided to pay Diana a visit when there was a witness, PC Whittaker. You found a hood and a face mask, dressed completely in black and drove to the Sheriffs' house. You were lucky when you arrived. There was a police car outside. You looked around for a way in and found the back windows open. So you went in and found my officer and Diana Sheriff. You hit PC Whittaker over the head and then killed Mrs Sheriff with a single bullet. Next, you left the gun behind to make it appear like another suicide. There were differences, though, and those were quite deliberate. Despite leaving the gun, your intention was to make very clear that this was a murder. It had to be because there was a witness to the fact that somebody else was in that property and whilst the intruder and Diana were the only conscious people present, Diana was shot. It did not fit in with the other suicide deaths and you did not want it to. It was vital that this was seen as a murder."

"Why would I want to do that?"

"Because if Mrs Sheriff's death was formally recorded as murder by person or persons unknown, you would seek to have your husband's death treated as murder as well. You needed his demise to be ruled as murder. That way you could claim the insurance money. Two million pounds."

Sergeant Adams, who has been fighting to stay awake throughout the interview, perks up at this comment. Elizabeth starts to cry.

Melville continues, "You needed a witness, and a police officer was ideal. However, that was also a mistake because the suicide killer works secretly and kills, in most cases, when he or she is alone with the victim."

Elizabeth replies through her tears. "My damned husband. I put up with his infidelity and with him bringing his conquests round to parade them in front of me just to humiliate me more. He always promised me I would live in luxury after his death. Then the silly sod gets murdered but by a killer who makes it look so much like suicide that nobody can be certain a crime has even been committed. I have nothing against Diana. She was a vast improvement on most of his bits of stuff. I tried so hard to make it identical to William, but you are right. There had to be a difference. A witness to confirm this one was definitely murder. What now?"

"You will make a statement admitting murder and assault on a police officer and then you will be formally charged. You will appear before magistrates tomorrow and I have no doubt you will be remanded in custody."

"This is almost a relief. I found it impossible to get Diana off my mind. Take me wherever I have to go next."

"Sergeant, can you find someone to take her statement? I will stay here with her."

*

Five minutes later, the officers are ready for the next task.

"That was a good trick recreating the murder. You got away with it once. You will struggle to make it two with Pomfrey," Sergeant Adams comments.

"We will see but one out of two is not bad. Two out of two is much better, though. Is she here?"

"Yes, sir. Interview room one. Sir, when this one is done, can I please go home?"

"I think there will still be one loose end to unravel but after that the answer is yes."

Shirley Pomfrey cuts a pathetic figure when they enter the interview room. She is slumped across the desk, crying quietly. She is wearing torn jeans and a shabby, dirty sweater. The effect is to make her look much older than twenty-one. As she lifts her head up, the letters "S-L-U-T" are clearly visible stamped across her forehead. Overall she looks broken.

CI Melville starts speaking, "Ms Pomfrey, I wish to ask you some questions about the death of Linda Taylor."

"Nothing to do with me," Shirley's voice is strained, and she speaks slowly and quietly.

"You have been read your rights, I believe. Do you want a solicitor?"

"Yes to the rights. No to the solicitor."

"What I am going to do is tell you what I think happened today. If I am wrong, please say so." Turning to Sergeant Adams, he adds, "Is this how she was when you met her?"

Adams nods and Melville turns back to Ms Pomfrey. "We have both seen the 'my life has been ruined' act now. So sit up straight, talk properly and let us see the real Shirley Pomfrey. The one who drives a car and goes on fifteen-mile walks with the local ramblers group."

Surpisingly, she does as the Chief Inspector requests. She sits up ramrod straight, rummages in her handbag and produces a pair of designer spectacles. She then finds a scarf in her bag and covers up her branding. When she speaks, her voice is clearer and louder with an angry undertone, "Get on with it. You have no damn right to drag me here late at night."

"The start of all this goes back eight years when you, Linda Taylor and Luke Turney were thirteen years old and at school together. There was a fight in which you were badly hurt by Linda. Sergeant Adams and myself assumed the fight was over Luke. You had him and Linda wanted him, but that is wrong isn't it, Ms Pomfrey?"

"My personal life has nothing to do with this."

"But it has and you know it. Love and sex have everything to do with this. Everyone assumed that Linda Taylor arranged the fight. If she won, she became Luke's girlfriend. If she lost, then you would continue to go out and sleep in with him. In fact, the arrangement was very different. You wanted the fight. Presumably, you had been going out with Linda before you moved on to Luke. Perhaps you decided you prefer girls or perhaps you were fed up with Luke. Whichever, if you won, you and Linda would get back together. If she won, you would stay away from her and remain with your boyfriend."

"Fuck you. Leave me alone."

"I think you believed Linda would let you win, so that you could be together again. But Linda, for whatever reason, knocked seven bells out of you. It was at this point that everything went wrong. You ended up in hospital, where they virginity tested you. The police charged you with sex offences and you still bear the scars of the punishment meted out to you." Melville stops, as Shirley Pomfrey starts crying again. She composes herself and he continues, "Linda got away lightly compared to you, as technically she was still a virgin. She was out, unbranded, within six months. She should have run straight back to Luke if the fight was actually about him. That was what Luke expected but it never happened. That puzzled me. She won the fight but never claimed her prize."

"She ruined my life. We had agreed that I would win the fight. I wanted shot of Luke, but he told me his father would arrange for me to be gang-raped if I dumped him. He wanted Linda and so did I. Until we started fighting I thought Linda wanted me. She just went crazy, tearing my hair out and eventually she started smashing my head into the concrete playground. I thought I was going to die. Some days I still wish I had."

"Did you leave Linda before the fight?"

"Yes. I was stupid. Luke was good at sex but wasn't interested in love or romance like Linda."

"You never went back to school and you had no contact with Linda or Luke until, I suspect, very recently. You stewed over your mistreatment for over five years, waiting. Waiting for a chance to get revenge. I am uncertain about what happened, but presumably you met up with Linda Taylor. You were genuinely damaged by your experiences but compared to Taylor you were doing well. She was drug-ravaged, old before her time and working as a prostitute. A terrible irony that she avoided men at school and ended up selling herself to them in order to buy drugs. How am I doing?"

"The only thing that got me through over two years of hell was that I would get even one day. I spoke to her parents and they said she moved out the day after she finished school and they had not heard of her since. I kept travelling to London but it was impossible. Just too many people. Then I saw in a paper that a Linda Taylor had been jailed for drug offences. I just knew it was her. I rang prisons, pretending to be a relative who wanted to collect her when she was released. On the day she came out, I drove to the prison. She got on a bus and I followed her into London. She ended up in some alley in Soho. There were other girls there. One of them gave her some sort of drug. I didn't feel safe there but I had seen enough to know what kind of life she led. I disguised myself as best I could and hung around. After a few days, I saw her having a row with a dealer. She didn't have enough money for what she needed so I joined in, bought some stuff myself and paid her shortfall. We got talking and I gave her my drugs as well as her own. She sort of went into a trance when she took too much. In the last week, I have helped her put a huge amount of drugs into her system. I got her used to obeying me when she went into a trance. I decided to strike today. I stole a car, which was easy because the key was in the ignition and the doors were unlocked. There has been so much in the papers about the suicide killings and their connection to Sara Molan. I could not believe my luck when armed police officers were assigned to guard Sara Molan. I met Linda as usual this morning, filled her full of crap and waited for her to go into a trance. Then I drove close to the house, helped her dress in the clothes I wanted her to wear and told her to drive round the corner and park behind the last vehicle. I gave her the gun and a facemask and told her to put on the mask, get out and walk towards the officer waving her gun in his direction. It worked a treat. Goodbye Linda. I thought it would be viewed as a threat to Sara Molan. I was shocked when Sergeant Hollis rang and then Sergeant Adams turned up but delighted when he offered me the chance to get back at Luke Turney as well. How did you get on to me?"

"There was one bullet in the gun. If Linda was after Sara Molan, why would she pick a fight with an armed officer? If she shot him, she had no bullets left. So, what was the point? She was clearly drugged and was in a trance. It did not fit in with the suicide murders. I looked at the victim and the fight stuck out to me. It seemed unlikely but sometimes the unlikely is the right solution. I want you to sign a confession and I will have you assessed by a psychiatrist. Personally, I think you need help rather than punishment and, hopefully, the experts will agree."

Moving outside, Sergeant Adams says, "I'm sorry, sir. She fooled me completely. Mind you, I did say she was mad."

"Don't feel too bad. She managed to fool Linda Taylor, who physically fought her just eight years ago. Whether she is clinically mad or not, she is another victim of Godwin and his legalised brand of sadism."

"Can I please go home now, sir?"

"Soon. One more thing for us to do."

Down in the basement of the police station, Melville leads the way to Luke Turney's cell, "Good, you are still awake. Luke, I have just managed to get Shirley Pomfrey to confess to killing Linda Taylor. I see no point in prosecuting you over historic sex offences when the only witness has admitted to murder. You are free to go and I am de-arresting you. I will get someone to drive you home. If Scarlet has killed your father, do us a favour and let Sergeant Adams and I get to sleep before you ring nine, nine, nine."

The Chief Inspector then turns to Adams, "Sergeant, leave your car here and get a taxi home. Put it on expenses.

Do not come in tomorrow. Thank you for all your help and patience." With that, they both finally head for home. In Sergeant Adams' case, after thirty hours on duty.

*

Two days later, they both return to work. Sergeant Hollis is very keen to see Melville. "This came yesterday," he says, thrusting forward a magnum of champagne. "It says on the card 'Many thanks' and your name is on it. What did I do?"

"Solved two murders and stopped me wasting months trying to link those two cases to the various suicides."

"I still do not know what I did."

"You told me the pieces didn't belong. Once I started treating them as completely separate to the suicide murders, it became clear who was guilty. Could not have done it without you."

"Well, I'll be damned. Thank you, sir."

"How did the two accused get on in court?"

"Elizabeth Marshall entered a plea of guilty and was remanded in custody. Shirley Pomfrey was sent to a psychiatric hospital for evaluation. The judge didn't even think she was capable of entering a plea let alone going to trial."

"She waited eight years to take revenge for losing a school fight that she instigated and she did it in the most convoluted and bizarre way imaginable. She actually managed to achieve murder by police. She's a long way from being sane. Hopefully, somebody somewhere can sort her mind out. At the moment, she is a danger to anyone who crosses her. I had better watch out when she is released. Can you tell Sergeant Adams to meet me outside in ten minutes and bring with him the address of the two bridesmaids at Sara Molan's wedding?"

"Yes, sir."

*

The journey is uneventful. The address is a flat in a run-down block in Camden. The front door is open and Melville and Adams soon find the right flat. They knock but get no reply. Melville pushes the door and it opens.

"Sergeant, you take upstairs."

There are two rooms downstairs, a large living room and a kitchen. The main room is untidy with magazines and empty bottles strewn around. The kitchen is filthy and it is hard to imagine any food being prepared amongst the mess. Melville opens a cupboard at random and finds a lethal cocktail of hard drugs and alcohol fighting for room. He thinks, "What a way to live."

His thoughts are interrupted by a shout from Sergeant Adams and he quickly goes upstairs.

The Sergeant is standing outside on the landing. He enters the nearest room and the Chief Inspector follows.

Taken aback by what he sees, Melville says quietly, "Good God."

Acknowledgements

I would like to thank Kathy, Ian and Sally, Clive and Dilys and Sue for their support and encouragement.

I would also like to thank Nicole for allowing me to use her name in various formats for characters in this novel on the strict understanding that they would be nice characters.

And thank you for your interest in my endeavours to Hannah, who is going to be a hugely successful writer herself one day very soon.

Finally, huge thanks to everyone at Troubador Publishing and Matador for their unfailing professionalism and help throughout this project.